The Heavenward Path

Also by Kara Dalkey

LITTLE SISTER

Kara Dalkey

The Heavenward Path

HARCOURT BRACE & COMPANY

SAN DIEGO / NEW YORK / LONDON

Copyright © 1998 by Kara Dalkey

Library of Congress Cataloging-in-Publication Data
Dalkey, Kara, 1953–
The heavenward path / Kara Dalkey.
p. cm.
Sequel to: Little sister.
Summary: Haunted by a broken promise to a powerful god,
fifteen-year-old Mitsuko again enlists the aid of a mischievous
shape-shifter who helps her learn to think for herself.
ISBN 0-15-201652-x
[1. Fantasy. 2. Supernatural — Fiction. 3. Japan — History —
Heian period, 794–1185 — Fiction.] I. Title.
PZ7.D1565He 1998
[Fic] — dc21   97-28940

Text set in Electra
Designed by Camilla Filancia

First edition
F E D C B A

PRINTED IN THE UNITED STATES OF AMERICA

To JANE YOLEN

because

The Heavenward Path

I seem to be gathering names.
I am Mitsuko, fourth daughter,
and my family is of the great
Fujiwara clan. Some call me
Little Puddle because of a
poem I wrote long ago at the
Imperial Court. When I
studied to become a Buddhist
nun, I thought I would take
some other name. But I doubt
that will ever happen now.
For a stone has fallen into this
little puddle, splashing it into
a new shape, erasing the clouds
reflected on its surface....

Ignorance

Is the hare blessed
who does not see the falcon's
talons above him?

𝒪T BEGAN WITH the wind. It was a warm, autumn night, late in Leaf-Turning Month, and I was in my room in the Sukaku Temple, where I had gone to study Buddhism. I was copying a long sacred poem, one of the sutras, by lamplight. I was in that delicious state of half-awakeness, when one hardly notices the movements of one's hand rubbing the brush against the inkstone or flicking the brush tip against the rice paper. I imagined myself approaching that state of being-and-not-being that the monks of the temple so highly prized.

But slowly I became aware of a soft hissing beyond the shōji sliding door beside me, a sound like the sea foam at Sagami Bay rushing up onto the shore. "It is merely the wind in the tall grasses," I told myself, and I tried to ignore it.

But the wind went on and on, growing louder. I almost

thought I could hear words in its whispers and moans. My skin began to prickle, and despite the seven layers of silk kimonos I wore, I shivered with chills. My hand trembled, and I had to set my brush down so that I would not ruin my work. There was a clattering on the roof tiles. "A mouse," I told myself. "Or a bird, or a bat." The sliding door began to shake and rattle, as if something was trying to get in. I was all too aware that the shōji was a fragile thing of only wood and paper, hardly a strong barrier between me and the monsters I imagined on the other side.

"Good evening," I said, my voice quavering. "Is someone there? Who is it?"

The wind whistled high and shrill among the roof beams, and the great temple bell intoned in the distance.

"Goranu?" I asked, feeling very strange. Surely this could not be the work of the tengu who had befriended me and helped me search for my sister's soul two years before. It was true that the shape-changing demon loved to play tricks on the pious and pompous, and it was true that I had made him unhappy when I'd told him I would not teach him the Way of the Buddha. He had wished to give up his immortality to be reborn a mortal human in another life, in the foolish hope that he might then be able to marry me. I had thought this an improper reason to seek the Heavenward Path, and I refused him. Yet surely he would not be so cruel as to frighten me this way.

But if not the work of Goranu, what else could this visitation be? I knew in my bones that it was no ordinary wind.

Old ghost stories came to my mind, and I picked up the paper with the sutra on it, clasping it close to my chest in hopes that the sacred words would protect me. *Sukaku Temple is holy ground*, I thought. *Only an extraordinary ghost or demon would have the power to enter here!* I backed away from the shōji and huddled in the corner, now imagining a creature beyond the door with enormous eyes and long fangs and many hairy legs, trying to scratch through the wood and paper.

But no such thing appeared. The wind hissed and droned on and on. The door rattled but never moved aside. The roof tiles clattered but did not fall in. *You are being foolish*, I told myself. *It is nothing and no one, after all.*

In time, weariness overcame my fear, and I crawled onto my sleeping mat and drifted off to sleep. This, however, brought no escape, for the wind followed me into my dreams. I had visions of mountain pines, their branches waving wildly, dark against a moonless sky. "Mitssssssssuko," the wind whispered. "Mitsssssssssuko. You promisssssssssed!"

A servant shook me awake the next morning, her face full of concern. "Are you all right, my Lady?"

I did not wish to seem foolish, so I said nothing about the wind or my dreams.

When I joined the other girls for the morning meal, for several daughters of Imperial Court nobles studied at Sukaku Temple, I asked, "Did you hear the wind last night? It was eerie, neh?"

They regarded me as though I were a fish served out of season. "I think I heard a little breeze," one of them said, "but, really, it was nothing special. Not enough to ease this autumn heat. You must have been imagining things."

Her answer unsettled me, and I vowed to say nothing more about it to anyone.

It was difficult to stay awake that day during the droning lectures of the monks. I was pleased when the sun set, at last, and I could try to get some sleep.

But the wind entered my dreams again, moaning in anger, hissing my name. When I awoke the next morning, I was relieved to see the sun, and yet already I dreaded the night to come.

So it went for the following few days. Each night my dreams were haunted by the wind, until, from lack of sleep, I could not speak or think or act without someone else prodding me. I am sure I became the subject of much whispering among the other girls. "She is pining for a lover," they doubtless said. Or, "She is going mad."

I was beginning to think so myself. My mood became worse when, in the following week, I heard that the temple well was drying up. And that a trade caravan bringing rice for the temple was robbed on the road and never arrived. And that a wing of one of the monks' dormitories caught fire, doing much damage.

I heard the other girls whispering that these things were my fault. Mad people were possessed by spirits, neh? And spirits bring bad luck. Had I not once been a friend of a tengu? In my wearied state, I began to believe the rumors and kept myself apart from the other girls, brooding over what I should do.

What could possibly have earned me this fate? I wondered. Had I offended some saintly spirit during my pilgrimages to the temples around Heian Kyō? Had I studied the sutras incorrectly? What sort of angry spirit could be haunting me?

My mother had died the year before. I found it hard to grieve, for I could hardly believe she was gone. I had not seen her when she was ill. They say shame befalls those children who do not visit their parent's deathbed, but the fever that took her was so swift, I had no chance to return to Heian Kyō. And I did not attend her funeral, for I had a very good reason for staying away from cemeteries. Surely I could not be blamed.

No, the angry spirit was not Mama-chan—I would know if it were she.

But what if, I thought with growing horror, *it is Great Emma-O, the Lord of Death, still angry that I once trespassed in his domain? What if he comes at last to punish me for my crime?* I was so agitated from this thought that I could scarcely move or speak.

On the eighth day of Long Night Month, I was summoned before Tadashi, the chief nun. She was a formidable woman, large and stern. Kneeling on the floor in her gray robes and cowl, she seemed immovable, eternal, wise: a mountain that had grown a human face. I knelt before her and bowed until my forehead was pressed against the reed mat beneath me. Tadashi regarded me for many long moments before she spoke.

"So. Lady Mitsuko. It has been a long time since I last spoke with you. Perhaps too long."

By this time, so little had I slept that I could hardly gather my thoughts. "Indeed, Holy One," I mumbled.

"Has all been going well with you? Are your studies proceeding to your satisfaction?"

I do not remember what I muttered then, but I did try to be polite. The afternoon was warm, and I was feeling very drowsy.

The nun gazed out through the bamboo blinds for a while, as if watching the birds who chirped in the side garden or the yellow leaves drifting down from the ginkgo trees. At last she said, "See how the tall grasses are shaken by the breeze. They tremble as we do, when pushed by greater forces. I doubt the grass sleeps much on windy nights."

So. She had heard about my sleeplessness and my fear of the wind.

"How old are you now, Mitsuko?"

"Nearly sixteen, Holy One," I managed to say.

"Of course. The perfect age. I asked to see you in order to let you know that a letter has arrived from your father."

I sat up then, for I feared that bad fortune had now befallen someone else in my family. "My father, Holy One?"

"Ah." She smiled knowingly. "Is it a wind from the Clouds

on the Mountain that makes you tremble? I thought it might be."

Tadashi was referring, of course, to the Imperial Court, at which my father was Minister of the Right. I was, indeed, afraid to return home, knowing what my father would ask of me. But I did not wish Tadashi to think the wrong thing, so I at last blurted out my true fears. "Oh, Holy One, forgive me. Some unhappy spirit chastises me in the wind and haunts my dreams. I fear, because of past transgressions, I may be bringing bad fortune to the temple and to my family."

Tadashi sighed. "It never ceases to amaze me how the young think themselves the center of the universe. What bad fortune?"

"The well," I said. "The fire. The rice merchants."

"Did you drink all the water in the well?"

"Um, no, Holy One."

"And did you steal the rice from the merchants?"

"Of course not!"

"And did you set the fire yourself?"

"No! But my dreams . . . surely I am possessed by a spirit who could do these things."

"Oh, I can believe you are possessed. The young are often possessed by forces they cannot control." She sounded secretly amused. "But although your family, the Fujiwara, is a powerful clan, I do not think you can yet dry up wells, or set fires and rob merchants from a distance."

I wondered if she had been listening. Could she not understand how serious this was? "The other girls think it is my fault."

"Tch." She waved a hand like a fan before her face. "I have heard their rumors that you have a tengu for a friend. Such vicious gossip girls tell about one another. I think such creatures are merely stories. I have certainly never in my life seen such a thing."

You probably have, I thought. *But tengu are shape changers*

and love to fool the pious, so you would not have recognized it.
I imagined Goranu in the guise of an old monk—a shape he
often took—capering about in front of her and almost smiled.
"No, Holy One. I do not think my dreams are caused by tengu."

"So, then. What are these dreams you keep speaking of?"

I told her of the wind and the voices whispering my name,
hissing about broken promises.

Again, Tadashi did not speak for many moments but stared
out at the little garden beside her room. "It is a curious thing,
how events follow one upon another," she said at last. "But I
think I know the significance of your dreams." She reached over
to the little lacquered chest beside her and pulled open the top
drawer. She took from it a folded piece of fine rice paper. "Here
is your father's correspondence. I received it just yesterday." She
handed the paper to me.

I recognized the crest on one side of the paper as I unfolded
it. Within was a withered wisteria blossom. The note read:

> *Will the Light of Heaven*
> *shrivel our fairest flower?*
> *Send my daughter home.*

"He wants me to return to Heian Kyō," I said, looking up
at her. "But I must not go, don't you see? I will bring bad
fortune to him."

The nun sighed again. "The only way you will bring him
bad fortune, Lady Mitsuko, is by staying here and stubbornly
refusing to do your familial duty. You are a Fujiwara. I served
at Court myself when I was young, and I know what is required
of a noble daughter. You must learn proper deportment and
serve the Imperial family. And find a husband."

I had known for a long time that my father would someday
ask this of me. After I had helped him free my mother, brother,
and sisters from Lord Tsubushima, he had shown great patience
in letting me follow the path of a Buddhist acolyte and pilgrim.

It seemed, at last, his forbearance was ending. "But my dreams—"

Tadashi leaned toward me and said sternly, "If any angry spirit haunts your dreams, Lady Mitsuko, it is doubtless that of an ancestor who is prompting you to get on with the important things in life."

I gazed at the floor, studying the fraying ends of the braided reeds in the mat beneath me. She misunderstood my dreams, but it would have been very rude to say so. "Is that what it might be?"

"It is the most likely, neh? I may have removed myself from the world, but one still hears things. You are the last daughter of your branch of the Fujiwara. Your clan has not fared well in these troubled times. There is much hope, among your clan, that you will marry well and preserve the status of your family."

I pulled at one of the reeds in the mat and twisted it around my finger until it hurt. "I had hoped," I said softly, "to preserve the honor of my family by becoming a nun like you, and going on pilgrimages, and saying the sutras so that my relatives might find a better life."

"I know," said Tadashi, her expression softening a little. "You are a pious girl, and the frivolities of Court can be hard to bear. But you are young, Mitsuko. You have many years ahead of you. And after your children are grown and their positions secure, then you may retire and cut your hair and read the sutras all day. Then may you seek the Heavenward Path. You have time."

Unless I die before that, I thought, though I dared not contradict one so eminent.

"I think," the nun went on, "the promise you have not kept is the promise all children owe to their ancestors. Because of the exalted history of your family, it is most important that you keep yours. You should go back to Heian Kyō, and soon."

I stared at the fading wisteria flower. I knew it was no disappointed ancestor who troubled my dreams. Whatever god, demon or spirit, whatever kami haunted me was something very old and very dangerous. But I dared not tell Tadashi this. "I understand, Holy One" was all I said.

Tadashi smiled again. "Ah, good. You are an unusual girl, Lady Mitsuko, but you are wise. I am sure you will do what is right. You may retire early this evening to get your rest. Perhaps your dreams will be more peaceful tonight, neh?"

"Thank you, Holy One," I said, bowing once more. "I hope so." I left her presence as gracefully as I could. But my feelings of anxiety did not pass, and my dreams that night were no different than before.

Three mornings later, I was summoned to go to the Outer Garden of the temple. My heart fell, for I feared it was an emissary from Papa come to ensure that I go home. But as I walked the stone path through the chill early-morning mist, I thought it strange: The Outer Garden pavilion was where visitors who were not Buddhist were received.

A kichō had been set up for me on the pavilion platform, and I sat on the cushion beside it. Clearly my visitor was a stranger, then. Had it been a relative, a curtain of modesty would not be necessary. Could my father have sent a suitor for me all the way to the temple? How embarrassing that would be! What would I do with him? I looked to make sure the edges of my wide kimono sleeves did not stick out beneath the curtain frame, for I did not wish to seem flirtatious. I was grateful the light was misty, so that my visitor would not see my shadow on the silk curtain. I tried to remember the advice of my eldest sister, Amaiko, on how to genteelly turn away men's attentions, but I had forgotten it. *I have no knowledge of proper things,* I thought, sighing. *And I don't really want to know them. I do not belong at Court.*

A lone bush warbler sang sadly in a nearby tree. The scents

of incense and wood smoke drifted on the air. The mist parted a little, and dim sunlight fell upon the pavilion as if the sun itself were hiding behind a screen of gray silk. It brought out the golden color of the chrysanthemums growing near me. The morning dew sat heavy on their petals, and I murmured:

> Oh, youth-giving dew,
> help me stay a child always
> free from worldly cares.

Someone sat on the other side of the kichō. He said:

> Chrysanthemums fade,
> but their dew-drenched glory stays
> ever young in memory.

It was the voice of an old man, someone familiar. "Dentō!" I said, as I remembered. I almost clapped my hands with joy.

"I am pleased you remember me, Lady Mitsuko," the old monk said, "though it has been many months since we last spoke."

"How could I forget one who helped my family when we were so troubled? It is good of you to come visit this insignificant one. But I do not understand why you are here. You could have come into the temple itself. You are of a Buddhist sect, neh?"

"Not every temple welcomes an ubasoku, even one of the Shingon sect, my Lady. My . . . appreciation of Shinto faith and provincial mountain rituals are frowned upon by some. And a Certain Personage in the temple might not approve of my speaking to you."

I assumed he meant Tadashi. Did he know her? I supposed that if one were old enough and wandered enough, one would eventually know everyone important. "Then I will not tell her.

I am pleased you are here, anyway. What has brought you to this out-of-the-way place?"

"Strange winds have wafted me down from the mountains," he said.

My breath seemed to harden within my chest. "Strange winds..." I gasped.

"Know you something of strange winds, my Lady?"

Ubasoku are said to have wizardly powers—perhaps he somehow knew my plight. Or perhaps the same kami haunted him. I had to confide in him. "Oh, Dentō, I need your help again! I have been troubled for many nights by dreams filled with wind. It whispers and moans, and calls my name, and tells me of a promise I have not kept."

"Indeed?" said Dentō. "I was referring to an ancient poem, but now I see there was purpose to my mutterings. So, what sort of spirit is this, and what promise have you not kept?"

I put my hands to my head as if to hold in my fears. "I do not know! In my dreams, I see pine trees waving against a dark night sky, but that is all."

"Hmm," he said. And "Hmmm" again. "How interesting."

"I am sure this spirit is angry with me and is bringing bad luck to Sukaku Temple."

"I assume this is not a prank of your tengu friend?"

I was surprised a moment, then remembered that Dentō had met Goranu during our troubles in the past. "No, it is not Goranu. I am certain of that."

"Ah. Well. It is a powerful kami who can trouble you within holy temple grounds, let alone bring bad luck there."

I wrapped my arms around myself, feeling very cold inside. Was he confirming my worst fears? "But a kami god or spirit lives in one place, neh? If I have offended one, it could not disturb me unless I am where it lives."

"Kami can travel, Mitsuko. Particularly this month, when it

is said they go to Izumo to gather together and discuss the world."

"So one of them has decided to miss the gathering and haunt me instead?" It was difficult to keep my voice steady.

"Wait, Mitsuko. Do not let your thoughts jump around like startled rabbits. Let us look closely at your dreams. You say that you see pine trees? You know, in my recent wanderings in the western mountains, I came upon some hunters who were distressed. It seems that they can no longer enter their favorite hunting grounds because of some disturbed spirit that now lurks there. They also mentioned pine trees...whose boughs danced when there was no wind. But that was in Tamba Province, which is far from here."

I sat up straight. "Tamba Province? But I have been there, Dentō."

"Have you? Ah, yes, that was where I first met your family. And tried to help your poor sister. Then you and she ran away."

"Just so. When Lord Tsubushima came for us and tried to make my family move to his castle, we fled into the mountain forest. And there we hid for the night in a ..." I felt suddenly as though the Buddha Himself had struck me, and I nearly fell over. The kichō screen wobbled as I leaned against it.

"Lady Mitsuko? What is the matter?"

"A kami shrine!" I gasped, and almost laughed with relief. "We hid in a kami shrine! It was just a little one, and in terrible condition, and I thought it was abandoned." Memories of that night came back to me. How my sister and I found the shrine, which looked like a little house, just when we could run no farther, and we took shelter in it. Dentō had given me sakaki leaves and rice paper on which prayers had been written, for protection. "I took your prayers and stuck them into the roof beams, and I promised...Oh, Blessed Amida!"

"Please, Mitsuko, go on."

"I promised the kami of the shrine that if it helped my sister and me, I would see that the shrine was repaired and that the kami would not be forgotten. Then Goranu and the other tengu showed up and befriended us and took us to their village."

"Ah. Which is what led to your family being reunited."

"Yes, and my sister healed. Oh, Dentō, the kami *did* help, and I have never kept my part of the promise. No wonder it is angry!" I buried my face in my wide kimono sleeves, not knowing if I should laugh or cry. *If it is not Lord Emma-O, then perhaps I and my family are still safe.*

"But you have your answer now," said Dentō. "The proper thing to do seems clear enough. You must keep your promise and repair the shrine."

I paused and stared at his shadow on the kichō curtain. "But—I cannot travel all the way to Tamba Province by myself and rebuild a shrine with my own hands. I was so much younger when I made that promise. Just a child, really. I didn't know what I was saying. You cannot be serious, Dentō."

"Serious? It is serious to the kami who speaks in your dreams, neh? Serious enough for it to dare the holy walls of Sukaku Temple."

I fidgeted with the edges of my sleeves. "But surely we can make the kami understand that such a thing is impossible."

"Impossible? Is this the same Mitsuko who bravely kept her sister out of the castle of Lord Tsubushima? Is this the same girl who wanted to storm the heights of Mount Hiei and order the warrior monks to properly bury her brother-in-law? The same girl who, if the tales be true, dared enter the realm of the Lord of Death himself?"

I wished he had not remembered that. I swallowed hard and wished the sunlight, which now was brightly burning the mists away, would hide itself again behind the clouds. "My father once told me that great battles were easier than the little bureaucratic problems he faced at Court. It is not so simple,

Dentō. And the girl who did all those things has...changed."
Where had my courage fled these past two years? Had I hoped
that by hiding among pilgrims in temples, I would never have
to face my past?

I didn't feel powerful, or important, or brave. It wasn't brav-
ery that had let me search for Amaiko's soul. Visiting the nether-
world had been Goranu's idea. I had merely traveled along and
done what I had to when I got there. I only dared visit the Lord
of Death because I loved my sister so.

"That Mitsuko has changed? Nonsense. She is merely sleeping, dreaming of the Buddha and the Life to Be. It is time to
reawaken to the world."

"But we are taught that the world is illusion," I protested.

"It is easy to think so, until you stub your toe on a rock,"
said Dentō. "Come now, you are not without resources. Are
you not a Fujiwara? With the most powerful clan in the Empire
behind you, what could you not do?"

"It is not so simple," I said again, twisting a strand of my
long black hair between my fingers. "It is because I am Fujiwara
that they may not let me do *anything*. I am too important
in...other ways. You are free to travel. I am not."

"Then you must convince your family of the importance
of your task. It is to you the kami calls. It is your duty to appease it."

"I seem to be gathering duties," I grumbled.

"We have them from the day we are born. That is gimmu,
neh? But you need not be crushed by such burdens, Lady
Mitsuko. Doesn't the porter or the stonemason become stronger
from the weight he must carry? As I see it, there is much to be
said for shouldering one's debts cheerfully and discharging
them well. The challenge invigorates the spirit, and helping
others brings grace to one's nature. Surely fulfilling your promise to the kami will further you upon the Heavenward Path."

This philosophy was somewhat different from what the monks of the temple taught about distancing oneself from the sin-filled world. No wonder the monks disapproved of Dentō.

"You know," he continued, "there is a rightness to this duty you must perform."

I turned and frowned at his shadow on the kichō. *Even he does not listen to what I say.* "Rightness? For a noble girl to rebuild a shrine?"

"How much do you know of your clan's history, my Lady?"

"Only the stories I heard as a child." Most of them had been about great wars and who married whom. I had not paid much attention to them.

"The Fujiwara have been powerful for many centuries, Mitsuko. They served the Imperial family even before the Capital was at Heian Kyō, before it was at Nagaoka. Even back when the Palace was in Heijo, the Fujiwara served at the Emperor's side. Your clan was called Nakatomi then, and their specific office was to serve and chant Shinto prayers before the Sacred Mirror. This was before the Way of the Buddha became known on these islands."

I sighed, losing interest in his words. I could not see what this history had to do with me.

As if he read my thoughts, Dentō moved closer to the kichō and said, "But the women of the Nakatomi were different than the Fujiwara are now. Many Nakatomi ladies were shamans and ubasoku-diviners and healers of great power—such as Queen Himiko of Yamatai."

"They were?" My hair started to stand on end, though I could not say why.

"Yes! And although such magically talented women have not been seen in the Fujiwara line for many, many years, I think at last one may have come forth again."

"Me?"

"Just possibly. This may be why the kami of the forgotten shrine is so angry. Your promise had sacred power, while one from an ordinary girl would not."

"Oh. I see." I pulled my kimonos tighter around me.

"I believe I have seen that shrine," Dentō said, "during my wanderings. If I am thinking of the right place, it is an odd little structure."

"Odd? How so?" As my family is Buddhist, I was not at all familiar with the different sorts of Shinto shrines.

"Normally, a shrine is placed in an impressive setting: near a waterfall, or a mountainside where there are beautiful views, or even an interesting boulder. Your shrine, if it is the one I think, had no such landmark. In fact, its setting is quite ordinary."

It had not seemed ordinary to me, but then it had been a haven amid the dark, forbidding pines. "Perhaps it was built to honor the kami of the whole forest," I suggested.

His shadow on the screen shook its head. "Had that been true, my Lady, a better location would have been found, and it would have been a more elaborate structure."

I tugged on my hair as if trying to pull thoughts from my head. "Well, perhaps the shrine is terribly ancient and devoted to something else, and the forest grew up around it."

"Ah. That is a very perceptive thought. I do recall there may be some historical significance to the place, but I cannot recall what it is."

I confess, I began to grow more curious about the strange little shrine and how a kami of great power might have come to reside there. A part of me had been feeling caged living in the temple dormitory, and I looked forward to traveling again. "You are right, Dentō. I am being too stubborn. Surely my family could help me repair a simple little shrine. After all, my sister Sōtoko lives near there now, with her new husband. I am sure they would know what to do."

"Ah. There is the brave Mitsuko I remember. And besides, if all else fails, you can always call upon your tengu friend for assistance, neh?"

"I suppose," I murmured, although I hoped that would not be necessary. I had asked so much of Goranu in the past, and given him so little in return.

"Your way is clear, then. You must go back to Heian Kyō to enlist your family's help."

"Will you come with me, Dentō, to help explain things to my father?"

"I wish I could, Mitsuko, but there is a village to the south of here haunted by sickness. I must go and perform cleansing rites, and perhaps learn the source and nature of the ailment to rid them of it."

"Oh." I was disappointed, but what could I say? I could not order him to choose one duty over another.

"But you are clever, Mitsuko, as well as brave. I am sure you will be able to manage things."

"I will do my best," I murmured. "Thank you, Dentō. I will remember all you have told me."

We said our good-byes then, but as his shadow vanished from the kichō curtain, I wished I could reach my hand through the cloth and grasp the hem of his jacket to keep him from going. Without his guidance, I feared I would be lost. I heard his footsteps departing on the garden flagstones, and soon I was alone. I hurried back to the temple to make my preparations. I sent Tadashi a note:

> Like grass in the wind,
>> this dutiful daughter bows.
> I will return home.

That night, my dreams were different. I saw a woman in many bulky old-fashioned kimonos, her long hair waving wildly about her, dancing in a forest of pines. She was shaking sakaki branches in her hands and chanting something I could not hear. I felt I had seen her face before—dimly glimpsed in the Land of the Ancestors. Again the wind entered my dream, but it was calmer than before. The pines did not whisper my name, and I slept better than I had in days.

Action

What a cheerful sound!
The turning of a carriage wheel
on the homeward road.

ONLY FIVE DAYS later, a carriage arrived from Heian Kyō to take me back to the Capital. The messenger bearing my letter to my father must have run like the wind! Twenty Guardsmen of the Inner Ward, looking splendid in their red capes, accompanied the carriage. It was one of my father's finest: black lacquered wood with red and gold cords woven into the latticework sides, the Fujiwara crest printed on the silk curtains, and a roof-canopy of carefully split palm leaves. The two oxen that drew the carriage had polished horns and shiny black coats, and were very well matched. Surely anyone seeing this procession would say, "There goes a lady of importance indeed!"

As I watched the servants loading my things into the carriage, Tadashi came up beside me. "So, Lady Mitsuko. Off to your grand future at last. I am sorry to see you go, for you have brought some noble grace to our provincial temple. I hope your journey home is safe and pleasant."

I bowed to her. "I thank you, Holy One, for allowing me to study here. I have learned much, and I hope to return someday." I looked back at the carriage and sighed. "Why did my father take so much trouble for me?"

Tadashi smiled. "A lady of the Good People is like a precious jewel, Lady Mitsuko. She must be surrounded by those things that display and enhance her quality. You must remember this when you begin your service at Court."

"I will, Holy One," I said, although it seemed I was more like a songbird being coaxed into a cage than a jewel. I allowed the guardsmen to assist me in getting into the rear door of the carriage, where another surprise awaited me.

"Hey, Little Puddle in the Clouds! Good to see you again!"

"Mochi?" I fell ungracefully onto the carriage seat in astonishment. It was, indeed, the rice cake girl whose family had taken me in when my father's house burned down. But she had changed. She now wore the many-layered silk kimonos of a servant in a noble household, but in a most displeasing arrangement. Even I knew that one did not wear the pink kimonos of spring over the gold ones of autumn. She had attempted to shave her eyebrows and stain her teeth with purple berries in the classic Court fashion. Such attempts at the noble ideal of beauty looked strange on her sun-browned face.

She tugged pridefully on her sleeves. "Not Mochi anymore. I hardly ever make rice cakes now that I serve in a great Fujiwara house. Now you may call me Suzume."

So, I was not the only one gathering names. Sparrow, however, was at least an appropriate name for her to take, as she was such a common little creature. It may seem harsh to say so, but I was annoyed with her. Not so much because she was taking on the airs of those more noble than she, but because she had changed. I had been used to her plain clothes and blunt ways—that was what I had liked about her. It was disturbing to see her so different. It was as though I had never really known her.

"Why must everything change?" I murmured as I tried to find a more comfortable position on the carriage cushions.

"What did you say?"

"Oh, pardon me. I said I am glad to see you well."

She had on a grin nearly as wide as her face. "This is so exciting, neh? Me, getting to ride like a grand lady through the streets of the Capital! You must show me the proper way to let my sleeves show from under the bamboo blinds. Do you let them hang out a little or a lot?"

I shuddered inside, for the arrangement of her sleeves was nothing to display proudly. "I am sorry, I have been at the temple so long, I have forgotten," I said. "Let us keep our sleeves inside and let people wonder which fine ladies are riding by."

"That's true, you Good People make a big fuss over ladies being mysterious. Very well, let them wonder."

The men outside closed the carriage door, and I heard the driver crack the ox-stick. The carriage lurched forward, nearly pitching Mochi—that is, Suzume—onto my lap. She scrambled back onto her seat giggling, and I began to fear that the trip might seem far longer than it ought.

"You know, your papa picked me especially to come meet you," Suzume said proudly.

"Did he?"

"Yes! Maybe he will arrange it so that I am your personal maid when you go to serve at Court, do you think? Imagine! Me living with the People Who Dwell Above the Clouds."

Surely, I thought, *Papa would not be so mad as to make Suzume my handmaid at Court.* As Tadashi said, the quality of a noblewoman is known by her surroundings, and a former rice cake girl who couldn't even dress right—and then I caught myself. Suzume and her family had been kind to me when others had turned away. And I was not intending to go to Court. There was the matter of the kami shrine to attend to. Who knew how long that might take? If I could convince my father that a life seeking the Heavenward Path would bring as much honor to the clan as marrying well, I might never have to go to Court at all.

But it would have been unkind to quash Suzume's dreams so. I smiled at her and said, "I thought you poor folk made fun of Those Who Live Above the Clouds and considered our way of life foolish."

"Oh, of course we do! Because we are jealous and want to live just like you. Or at least have your nice things." She fussed with her sleeves as if not sure what to do with her hands.

"But noblewomen and their servants have to hide behind screens and kichōs. Surely you would miss being able to wander the city freely?"

"Heh. Being pinched and leered at by drunk old men, and having to watch out for thieves, and being tired all day from carrying rice cakes all over town? No, thank you. A life behind screens writing poems seems like heaven to me. By the way, the gossip behind the walls is that your papa already has a husband picked out for you."

"Does he?" My spirits sank further.

She leaned forward and said in a loud whisper, "Someone very high ranked, I hear."

"Oh." I hid my face behind my wide sleeves as if in embarrassment but actually to hide my dismay. My father probably had chosen some withered old government minister to whom Papa owed a favor. I did not know much about political matters, but I did know that girls often found their way of life sacrificed for them.

Suzume patted my arm. "Oh, don't worry. Mama says husbands can be annoying sometimes, but they're better than starving."

"That is not a high recommendation," I said with a sigh.

Suzume shrugged. "It is if you have ever starved."

Truly the common folk see the world differently.

It took three days to travel from Sukaku Temple to the Imperial Capital of Heian Kyō. We stopped in small but well-kept inns along the way. Already I found myself missing my life at the temple; the sonorous chanting of the monks, the booming of the great bell. It had been so peaceful there. Now my life was about to suffer great changes once more, becoming as different as winter is from summer.

We entered the Capital through the Rasho Mon, the southernmost gate, and proceeded straight up the great thoroughfare of Suzaku Avenue. I peered out through the carriage curtain to see the tall willows lining the street and the throngs of people, on foot or on horseback or in carriages like mine. Every sound and smell reminded me I was home again.

Suzume knew the streets well from her life as a rice cake girl, and gleefully gave me a running account. "Oh, now we are passing the place where the bandit called Oni robbed five noblemen in broad daylight! Oh, and over there is Zurui, the fishmonger who always charges too much for his clams. Oh, and now we are passing the silk weavers—they always sell their worst cloth to lowly folk. They keep the best for people from the Palace. Hah! Guess I'll get to wear their finest wares after all, neh?"

She really was becoming quite tiresome. I remembered how, before my adventures began, I had lived as noble girls do: closeted behind blinds and screens, rarely leaving my father's house. I had been desperate for news of the outside world, and Suzume would sometimes come by on her rounds and tell me what she had seen. Now, however, my duties weighed so heavily upon me that such ordinary details seemed foolish, unnecessary. *Suzume isn't the only one who has changed,* I thought.

We pulled off Suzaku Avenue into the neighborhood that is known as the Third Ward. Here I became disoriented, for my father had gotten a new house after I went on pilgrimage and Mama died, so I did not know where we were going.

At last, the carriage jolted with a great bump as we passed over a gate threshold beam, and we stopped. I peered out through the window curtain in the back door. Behind us was a huge, elegant wooden gate with the Fujiwara crest on it, set into a high wall of white stone.

"We're home!" said Suzume.

But I had never lived in this house, so it was not home to me.

Our escorts unhitched the oxen and led them away, while others opened the door at the front of the carriage and helped us climb out. Suzume went first, which was proper. I had to remind myself to cover my face with my sleeves as befits a modest noble lady. Truly I had lived too long at the temple to be comfortable with courtly manners.

I was guided into a large, beautiful room. Its floors of polished cypress gleamed. It was furnished with cushions covered with gold silk, and Chinese screens depicting dragons in the clouds. All was very elegant. Here and there I recognized a go table or a carved chest that had been in my childhood home. But despite their presence, I felt like a visitor in a stranger's house. As I looked around, I realized how much I missed Mama-chan. She would not have decorated her northern pavilion like this—it would have felt more welcoming, less imposing.

The blinds were rolled up, allowing me to view one of the mansion's gardens. Close by was a cherry tree that had already lost half its leaves. No doubt it had been a splendid tree when blossoming in spring, but now it seemed rather dowdy.

I thought:

> Sad is the cherry
> in autumn. Sad is the
> pilgrim in silk robes.

Servants hurried in to give me a feast—or what seemed like a feast after the spare food I had been used to at the temple—rice with shredded daikon root, and baked fish with carrots and garlic, and some cakes made from melon and walnuts. But I could eat very little. I was trying to plan how I would ask my father for help repairing the shrine. Surely once he knew what bad fortune would befall us if I did not, he would provide all the assistance he could.

Just then, a young boy of six or seven entered the room, brandishing a wooden sword. He looked familiar, and then I realized who he must be. "Yūshō?"

He stopped and stared at me. "Who are you?"

"I am your sister Mitsuko. Don't you remember me?"

"Oh, now I remember! They told me you'd be coming."

My little brother was much changed since I had last seen him, two years before. "You've ... grown."

"So have you." He plopped down beside me. "Why haven't you come to visit us in so long?"

"I have been very far away. At Sukaku Temple."

"Papa told me. Did you like it at the temple? Did they teach you fighting like the monks on Hiei-zan?"

"No." I laughed. "We learned that is not the way to the Heavenward Path."

"Heh. A temple for cowards. I'm going to join the Palace Guards when I grow up. My friend Reigi says his papa can get

me a good position when I'm old enough. Then I can fight off
bandits and drive away demons on New Year's!"

"I am sure you will do very well," I murmured. I imagined
Yūshō in a battle with Goranu, and I suspected the tengu would
win. It almost made me smile.

"Your ambition is beneath you, Yūshō," said our father,
sweeping in, wearing his grand black robes and tall hat. "You
will do better than the Palace Guards. You should plan to become a fine general one day, and lead armies."

Yūshō stood up and proudly stuck out his chin. "I will if
you say so, Papa-san."

"Good. Now get to your studies. I have important things to
discuss with your sister."

"Yes, Papa-san." Yūshō bowed and ran out of the room.

I bowed to Father, too, and said, "It is good to see
you again." Suzume once told me how surprised she was at
the formality in the Good People's families. But are we not
taught to show respect for our elders? This is the way I have
always known things, and I cannot imagine being any other
way.

Papa knelt on a cushion near me. He seemed thinner than
before, and though his gladness shone through his eyes, there
was a tightness in his face that disturbed me. "And you,
Mitsuko. I am glad to see you are well. It pleases me that you
returned so soon after I sent my letter. I had been worried that
your thoughts were drifting so far from worldly things that you
had forgotten your family."

"I could never do that," I said, even though the strictest
Buddhist teachings require that the seeker do exactly that. "It
was important that I come home right away."

"Just so. You understand that your duty is important. I always knew you were a smart girl. How was your life at the
temple? Did they treat you well?"

I didn't have much to tell him. Life at the temple was

simple and dull—it was meant to be, so that one could concentrate on prayers and meditation.

"Well," said Papa, "your life will become much more interesting now. You will make quite an entrance at Court. I have been planning it carefully. You will be accompanied by only the finest furnishings and servants."

So much for Suzume's hopes, I thought, a little sadly. "Papa, if you please," I said hurriedly, for I feared I might not get another chance, "there is something I must ask for before I am sent to Court."

"Of course! Ask what you will. Would you like some new kimonos? Or a specially painted screen? Perhaps a bronze Chinese mirror? Nothing shall be withheld from you."

This heartened me. I took a deep breath and stared at the floor and began. "Nothing like that, Papa. Do you remember I told you about running away with Amaiko when we were going to be taken away by Lord Tsubushima's men? And we ran off into the forest and took shelter in a kami shrine. While there, I promised the kami of the shrine that I would see that the shrine was repaired if the kami would aid us. And the tengu came, and we were rescued, but I forgot about the promise to the kami. Now the kami is angry with me and is bringing bad fortune, and I have got to see that the shrine is repaired or something terrible will happen!"

When I looked up, Papa was scowling. "What is this nonsense? What drivel did they fill your head with at the temple?"

"It is not nonsense, Papa! The priest Dentō, who helped us in Tamba Province, told me so. You don't want me to bring dishonor and bad fortune on our family, do you? Surely it would be a simple thing to have the shrine repaired—it is close by the mountain lodge where Sōtōko and her husband now live."

"Simple? What can you be thinking, Mitsuko? I do not own that land. It is owned by Lord Tsubushima, and he would be responsible for the shrine. I have no wish to owe him any favors by asking it of him. But you are still a child, and I should not expect you to understand the politics of the wider world. Put off these foolish thoughts. Besides, we are a Buddhist family. What have we to do with Shinto shrines?"

"Dentō says that when we were the Nakatomi, Shinto was important to our family."

"That was long ago and has nothing to do with us now."

I noticed then that his hands were trembling. "What is wrong, Papa?"

"You. It is you who are wrong. I thought you understood the importance of what is expected of you, but I see I may be mistaken." He stood and began to pace the room. "We are Fujiwara. Our clan has been called 'the shadow cast by the Sun that is the Emperor.' We have served the Imperial family for centuries, our power in the Empire unwavering."

"I know this," I said softly.

He turned and glared at me. "Do you? Yet you want to go running off to temples and kami shrines when the future of your family is at stake? I see that perhaps I have been too lenient with you, and you have become stubborn and spoiled."

I became frightened by this change in him. What could possibly be disturbing him so? Were not my older sisters Amaiko and Kiwako already at Court, already in positions for favorable marriages? Why was his anger focused on me? Or was this also a sign of the kami's curse? I bowed where I sat, placing my forehead on the cool wood floor. "Please, Papa-san, I meant no disrespect. I had no idea I could possibly be so important."

This seemed to calm him. With a sigh, he said, "That is better. Perhaps you have been so shut off from the world that you are not aware of the state of things. The position of our clan is...not as secure as it once was. Branches of our clan squabble among one another for petty promotions. Other clans, jealous of our power, are trying to slip into the cracks. Even barbarians like Lord Tsubushima have the temerity to threaten and posture from the provinces."

It was frightening to hear Papa talk like this, but I still could not imagine what such politics had to do with me.

"However, an opportunity has arisen," Papa continued. "One that we ignore to our peril. Not long ago, your uncle the Chancellor informed me of one who seeks a wife. One who is closely related to the Emperor and could possibly be in line for the Chrysanthemum Throne someday. Many families with daughters of quality will be approaching him. But we have already decided, Mitsuko, that you should be the one to marry Prince Komakai."

I sat bolt upright then, in shock. I had not been so shut off from the world as to not know who Komakai was. "But Papa, he is only ten years old!"

"Eleven, actually, and that is not an unusual age for boys of the Imperial line to look for their first wife. Don't you see, Mitsuko? It is important that you be that first wife, and that you bear him sons. If Komakai should rise to the throne, then Fujiwara blood will stay in the Imperial line. If Komakai himself does not become Emperor, it is possible one of his sons may. Things happen in this uncertain world.

"However, if you do not marry Komakai and some other noble family arranges a match, then we have lost that opportunity, among others already lost. Your failure will only add to the Fujiwara's decline." He turned his back to me and stared out through the window blinds.

"But what about Amaiko or Kiwako? They have been at Court a while and are much better skilled at courtly things than I am."

"Amaiko is too old. And Kiwako...has developed an

unfortunate reputation. She is thought too frivolous. No, Mitsuko. It must be you."

I felt all my hope and courage flow out from me then. It was no wonder my father thought the shrine unimportant when the future of our family's fortunes weighed so heavily upon him. I wished I could make him see that this, too, might be the vengeance of the kami, and that would mean the shrine was of the greatest importance. But I knew he would only think me mad or possessed, and it would just upset him further. "Please forgive me, Father," I said. "I understand now."

"Good," he grumbled. "Then I will hear no more talk about shrines or any other such nonsense. Tomorrow you will move to your sister Amaiko's quarters beside the Palace, and she will teach you those customs and qualities you need to know before you are formally presented at Court. I will send word to Komakai that he will meet you soon, and, I hope, you will charm him so that he will desire no other companion but you. Think on this and prepare yourself." With no further words, he stalked from the room.

I slumped down onto the floor, hopelessness filling me. I had no idea how I would "charm" an eleven-year-old boy. The thought of marrying one disgusted me. I was quite unprepared for such a life. Papa was right to be worried.

But who knows how much misfortune would befall our family if I could not get the shrine repaired? Perhaps, if I married, I could convince the Imperial family to repair the shrine, but how many years would *that* take? Emperors were not known for swift action.

As I lay with my cheek against the cool wood floor, a horrible realization grew within me: I was going to have to disobey my father. I was going to have to disappoint my clan and perhaps ruin my family's chances for advancement. A part of me wondered how I could dare do such a thing; I might become an outcast, disinherited, my name only whispered in curses at

Court. But another part knew that I had to act before I was caged within the Palace walls.

That night, before I went to bed, Suzume pestered me with questions. "So? When do you go to Court? Who is it he wants you to marry? Will you take me with you?" It was impossible to ignore her.

"Papa wants me to marry a child, an eleven-year-old prince," I grumbled at last. "Truly it is, as they say, a woman's fate to wet her sleeves with tears a thousand times."

"It is also said," Suzume argued, "that a woman's will can shatter stones. You Good People give up too fast. You can easily boss around a boy of eleven. You can teach him to do what you like. And if he beats on you, it won't hurt as much, neh?"

I stared at her, shocked. "Court gentlemen do not beat their women."

"They don't? Another good thing about you People Above the Clouds. I hope I can find a husband among you."

"But Suzume..." No, I could not disappoint her.

"What about your shrine? Maybe when you marry, you can get your new husband's family to fix it as a wedding present."

"Perhaps."

"Ah. You have some other plan. Well, if you need any help, just ask me. You're brave, but you need somebody sensible like me to steer you right."

"I hope it will not come to that. If you please, I am very tired and would like to sleep." In truth, I could not stand her common chatter any longer. I climbed onto the sleeping platform and blew out the lamp.

"I understand, Lady Puddle. Big days ahead, neh? Sleep well." She picked up a lit taper and walked noisily out of the room, sliding the shōji shut behind her.

But I only pretended to go to sleep. When I could no longer hear her footsteps, I sat up again and found a narrow ebony box that I keep with my treasured things. I opened the box and took from it a long black feather. I then lifted up the shutters that led to the garden beside my rooms, and I slipped outside.

The garden was unfamiliar to me, so I stumbled and tripped on stones and bushes. If anyone had caught me, I would have claimed that I had gotten lost while seeking to do a necessary thing. But I was quite alone.

When it seemed I was far enough from the house to not be heard, I took the feather from my sleeve and said, "Goranu."

For a long time, nothing happened. A cold night breeze ruffled my kimonos, and I hugged myself for warmth. "Goranu?" I said again, a little louder.

There, against the starry black sky, I saw an even darker shape move across the stars, across the gray face of the moon. The shape of a large black bird. It circled down, closer and closer, until it landed behind some tall plum trees nearby.

I took a few steps closer toward the trees. "Goranu?"

He emerged onto the path, now in the shape of a young man wearing a black jacket and trousers, and with a very long nose. "So. Little Puddle," he said. "You've changed residence. I couldn't find you for a while. Did they kick you out of the temple because you refused to teach Buddhism to one who asked it?"

"Please don't be unkind, Goranu," I said, though I had expected him to be. "I know I have no right to ask anything more of you, but I am desperate." Long ago, I had tried to explain to Goranu that I could not bear to teach him the sutras because, since he is a demon, it would kill him painfully. Even though it might mean he would find a better life on the next turn of the Wheel, I could not face hurting him so.

"Heh. The Little Puddle has gotten herself in trouble again, and she thinks, *Hey, I know this silly tengu who will do anything I ask, if I trick him into believing I will teach him the sutras.* Well, I am a tengu, and I know tricks, and I am wise to yours.

I have heard mortals say that girls are untrustworthy, and now I know they speak the truth."

I pulled my hair in frustration. "Please, Goranu, stop! I know I have been horrible to you, and I am so very sorry. I just didn't want to see you hurt. But I would not have called on you if I did not need you."

"Hah. So. As long as I am here, tell this silly tengu what your problem is so I can laugh at you some more."

So I told him about the dreams and the shrine.

"Ah," he said. "That is bad. It is a dangerous thing to upset a kami. Now you see the trouble it brings not to keep your promises."

"I had forgotten the promise!" I wailed, and then quieted, for I realized there were people sleeping not far away. "I was just a child, and cold and frightened. I wasn't even sure a kami was listening."

"Tch. Then why did you make the bargain, eh? That is no excuse."

"But I want to set it right, now that I remember. My father won't help me. He wants me to go to Court immediately and marry an eleven-year-old boy."

"Hmmm." Goranu walked, chin in hand, back and forth in front of me. "Marry a little boy? No, that does not seem right at all. You mortals are beyond understanding sometimes."

"Yes," I sighed. "So, please. If you could just fly me to the mountain lodge where my sister Sōtōko now lives, that would be enough. The shrine is on Lord Tsubushima's land, and her husband is Lord Tsubushima's son. Surely they can help me. Will you do just that one thing for me?"

"Why should I?"

"Because...because you are the only one who can—" I could not speak any longer then, as tears were flowing from my eyes and my words caught in my throat. Unable to help myself, I wept into my sleeves.

Goranu sighed then, too, and said, "Stop that. Stop it right now. So, so. I am just a silly tengu, after all."

"Then...you will fly me to Tamba Province?"

He faced me squarely and said, "You know my price."

I wiped my face and realized it was no use trying to shelter him from suffering if he was determined. "I...I have the Lotus Sutra that I copied out in my own hand while at the temple. I will give it to you if you take me to Sōtōko. Will that suffice?"

"In your own hand?" he said, softly. "That would be a treasure worth flying to Ch'ang-an for. Bring it, and I will take you wherever you wish."

I did not understand why a copy would be so important to him, but I quickly fetched the scroll from my things, tucked it into my sleeve, and returned to him in the garden.

Goranu was again in bird shape and squatted down so that I could climb onto him. I crawled over his wing and onto his back, feeling happier than I had been in a long while.

"Oof! You've...grown, Little Puddle. Or you are heavier than I remembered. Hang on." He ran a few steps down the garden path, flapping his big black wings as hard as he could.

I dug my fingers into his feathers and savored their musty scent. It was so good to be flying with him again.

Goranu leaped into the air, and I thought I saw, as he passed over the house, Suzume standing on the veranda, watching us. *I hope she does not run and tell Papa*, I thought. *But there is nothing to be done for it now.*

How wonderful that night was! The lanterns of Heian Kyō glimmered below us like thousands of fireflies gathered in one place. The land round about was darker than the darkest silk. The stars above us were bright as sunlight glinting off water. The moon glowed like a silver mirror. As I lay between Goranu's great beating wings, I wished the flight would last forever.

But after an hour or two, we at last descended into the mountains of Tamba Province. I caught a whiff of pine-scented wind that made me shudder.

"Hang on," said Goranu. "This may be a rough landing."

I wrapped my arms around his neck. With several jarring bounces, Goranu finally stopped in front of the gate of my sister's mountain lodge.

"Uk. You can let go of me now," said the tengu in a slightly strangled voice.

Reluctantly, I let go of his neck and slid down his back to the ground. I took a little time to adjust my kimonos and smooth my windblown hair. When I at last turned to enter the lodge, Goranu, in human form again, blocked the gate.

He held out his hand. "Your payment?"

"Ah. Yes." Though it made me sad, I took the rice paper scroll from my sleeve and handed it to him.

Goranu began to take the scroll as if it were made of gold. Suddenly, it gave off a red glow. "Ow!" said the tengu, and he dropped it on the ground.

"Oh no! I should have realized," I said. "The sacred words will burn you."

"I will still take it with me," Goranu growled, shaking his hand and sucking on his fingers.

"Let me tuck it into your belt, so it will not hurt you."

"It will still be against my skin and feathers."

Not knowing what else to do, I removed my outermost kimono. I still had six other kimonos underneath, and Papa had said he'd buy me new ones, after all. I wrapped the scroll in the kimono so that it formed a thick bundle. "There, that should help." I gently reached over and pulled on Goranu's belt sash and tucked the bundle into it.

He breathed a soft, shuddering sigh.

"I'm sorry. Did that hurt you?" I looked up. His face was very close to mine.

"No, Mitsu-chan," he whispered down at me. "All is very well."

"Oh. Um."

"Um. You may let go of my belt now."

"Oh. Forgive me." I let go of his belt and took a step back. I did not want Goranu to leave. I did not want him to read the sutra and die. But I could think of nothing to say that would stop him. Already his fingers were sprouting feathers. He lightly touched my face and then took off running down the Western Road. In a moment, he was in the air, once more a darker patch of night against the shining stars.

New Inclinations

The little stream is
blocked by fallen leaves. Ah! It
can flow a new way. . . .

$\mathcal{A}$FTER GORANU's departure, I stared at the gate in the garden fence and wondered what to do. It would be foolish to stand out there shouting like a street vendor, so I pushed gently on the gate. It swung inward with only a faint squeak.

The house was on a steep hillside to my left. Bright lantern light shone through the translucent rice-paper-and-wood walls. *They have done much to repair this house,* I thought. *It looks almost pleasant.*

By the dim light, I could see that the tall weeds that had hidden my escape with Amaiko had been cut down and a garden had been planted with a pleasant graveled path winding through it. I heard footsteps on the veranda of the house, and I glanced up.

A woman walked there, but she was dressed very strangely.

Instead of the many layers of kimonos, she wore Chinese trousers and a long jacket that was slashed at the hip. Her hair was tied back with a strip of cloth. She did not seem to see me. She went to the veranda railing and held out her right hand, which was wrapped in leather. "Ki-ki-ki-ki-ki-ki!" she called out in a high-pitched voice.

Its wings only whispering, a hawk flew out of a nearby pine tree and landed gently on the woman's wrist. She turned toward me as she fed the bird something, and I recognized her.

"It is Sōtōko!" I said to myself. "So I am not the only Fujiwara who has charmed a feathered creature to do my bidding. Perhaps it is a family talent."

Suddenly both my arms were grasped by large hands.

"So, what have we here? I think we've caught a little trespasser!" said a gruff, bearded man on my left.

"A servant trying to imitate her betters, I'll wager," said a gruff man with bad teeth on my right.

"No I'm not!" I said, struggling with them. "I am Fujiwara no Mitsuko, and if you are wise you will let go of me!"

"Oh, a *Fujiwara*, are you?" said the man on my left.

"Walked here all the way from Heian Kyō, did you?" said the man on my right. Neither of them made any sign of letting go.

"No. I flew here."

"Oh!" The man on my left said with a knowing nod at the other man. "She *flew* here."

"What is all the noise down there?" asked Sōtōko from the veranda.

"Sōtōko!" I called up to her, no longer caring about embarrassment. "It is me, your sister, Mitsuko! Tell your guards to let me go!"

"Mits—" Sōtōko set the bird on a nearby perch and hurried to the end of the veranda. She ran down a flight of wooden stairs and came down the garden path to me. She put her hand under my chin and turned my face toward the light. "It is Mitsuko! Mitsu-chan, what miracle is this? You two, let go of her! She is no common criminal. We did not hire you to protect our house from our own family!"

Immediately, the two men released me. "You could have told us, my Lady," grumped the one on the left, "that you expected family visitors."

"She was alone, without the retinue of a noblewoman," complained the other. "How were we to know she was of your esteemed clan?"

"Surely you must be blind," said Sōtōko, "to have not seen the carriages and cohort of the Fujiwara."

"But Lady," said the first guard, peering through the garden gate, "the road is empty."

"It is true, Sōtōko," I finally said. "I am here alone. A tengu flew me here."

The guardsmen backed away, waving paper talismans before their faces. "Tengu!" they cried.

"Come," said Sōtōko, extending her hand to me. "You can explain all this where it is lighter and warmer, and where there is better company."

I allowed her to lead me up to the mountain lodge. As we went past the hawk on its perch, it screeched at me. "I am pleased you were still awake," I said to Sōtōko. "I don't know what I would have done if you had not been here to see me."

Sōtōko laughed. "Our household is quite unlike our father's home in Heian Kyō. We keep very odd hours here, and sleep and rise when we please."

How different the house looked from when our family had first taken refuge there. The walls had been repapered, and the wood beams and floors polished. The rooms were well-lit with lamps and lanterns, and adorned with sturdy chests and sword racks. I had to gasp in revulsion, however, when I saw the animal skins laid out on the floor as rugs.

"I know," Sōtōko said. "It is a trial to Buddhist sensibilities, neh? Lord Tsubushima wanted Court ladies as wives for his sons in hopes we would teach them civilized ways. But I fear I have changed more for my husband's sake than he for mine. But it is not all bad," she added as she pulled out from a chest of drawers a silk cushion for me to sit on. "Riko doesn't demand that I hide behind curtains, and I have learned many new things."

"Like how to call a hawk?" I asked.

"So you saw that? Yes, and guess what else? He gave me a horse of my very own!"

"What an unusual sort of pet," I said. "You don't let it in the house, do you? And it cannot sit upon your lap. All one can do is ride them. I know Lord Tsubushima made you ride one at your wedding, but surely your husband does not expect a noble lady such as you to want to do such a lowly thing."

Sōtōko laughed again. "But that is exactly what I do with the horse. Riko and I often go for rides in the woods nearby. It is very pleasant."

"Amazing!" I said, half in shock, half in admiration. "You have nearly become a barbarian yourself."

Just then, a young man, small and muscular, with a trimmed beard, sauntered in. "What is this?" he asked with a grin. "We have guests, and you did not tell me, Sōtōko?"

"Only one guest, Riko, and her visit was a surprise to me. This is my sister, Mitsuko, come all the way from Heian Kyō. Mitsuko, this is my husband, Tsubushima no Riko."

I held my sleeves up in front of my face, but he said, "No, no, there will be none of that formality in my house. You are family, and therefore I may see you, neh?"

I glanced with uncertainty at Sōtōko, then slowly lowered my arms. "As you wish, my Lord."

"None of that, either. You may call me Riko. Everybody

does. So, where is the rest of your party? Did your servants get quarters and your horses get stabled?"

"I came alone," I said. "There is no one with me."

Riko's grin fell, and he stared at me. "Alone? Up the Western Road? Impossible. Any lone travelers would fall prey to highwaymen or the warrior monks of Mount Hiei."

I sighed, remembering just such an attack on my family two years before. "Of course, but I did not face such dangers. I flew here on a tengu's back."

"Oh." Riko seemed to turn a little pale, and he rubbed his beard. "Yes, your father's skill at sorcery is renowned. I will never forget the day Sōtōko and I were married—the dragons in the clouds and the army of black-armored horsemen who turned into birds. Naturally, your father could send you here on the wings of a tengu."

Actually, it had been I who talked the tengu into creating the illusion of an army on the day of Sōtōko's wedding, and King Ryujin who had sent the sky-dragons, but I did not contradict Riko. After all, it might be better for my father's diplomacy if he were thought to be a great sorcerer. "Of course," I said.

"Well, then. There must be some weighty reason for him to send you to us."

"I have an important reason to be here, yes. I...we need your help with what will, to you, seem a very small matter."

"Let us hear it, then," said Riko with an expansive sweep of his arm. "I will be glad to lend assistance to the great Fujiwara."

Hope began to fill me, and I knew I had done the right thing. "There is a shrine to the south of here, in the forest. It is only a little shrine to a Shinto kami, but it sheltered my sister Amaiko and me during our...troubles two years ago. I...my father, in gratitude to the kami, wishes to repair the shrine, for it was in very poor condition."

Sōtōko gazed at me with a curious frown. I hoped she would not question me, for I did not want to tell her I was lying. I wondered how many times I would have to copy the Lotus Sutra in penance for my falsehoods.

"You are right," said Riko. "That should be simple enough. Scarcely a day's work for me and some of my men. I will be happy to oblige your father in this way. I think I even know the shrine you mean. Some of the hunters around here claim it is haunted."

"Yes, that is the one," I said happily. "No doubt the kami is upset because its shrine is so poorly kept, and that is why it haunts people nearby."

"All the better, then, that we should fix it!" said Riko. "We'll leave first thing after breakfast tomorrow. Will that suit your father?"

"Yes," I said, bowing low to hide my smiles. "That will suit splendidly."

I slept well that night in my sister's house, though the air was more chilly than I was used to. My dreams were peaceful, but I had the sense of something waiting...out there in the dark forest.

We rose before dawn and ate with our breath steaming out of our mouths. I tried to ignore the fact that Riko and Sōtōko were eating eggs. I had only onion-and-radish soup, but it tasted very good on a cold early morning.

After breakfast, Sōtōko took me down to the newly built stable and proudly led her horse out. It was a short, shaggy, coarse-haired creature, but I praised it highly for her sake. As servants put the saddle on, Sōtōko said, "You will ride with me."

"But I don't know how!" I protested.

"Surely a girl who rides on the backs of tengu can ride a simple horse."

"It isn't the same thing. You can recline on a tengu's back

as if it were a cushion. Horses have no feathers to grab on to."

"You will have to hold on to me. And grasp the horse between your legs."

This seemed very unladylike, and I said so.

"Hmph. You are beginning to sound like Amaiko. Do you want to go to your shrine or not?"

Once I would have found the comparison to our eldest sister complimentary. Now it stung. "I am not nearly so stuffy."

"Good. Come on, then." She led the horse over to a large garden stone. Sōtōko stepped up onto the stone and from there easily swung one leg over the horse's back to sit on it. I tried to do the same, but my many layered kimonos, so elegant when one is just sitting, were distinctly in the way. Finally, one of the guardsmen had to come up and grab me by the waist and set me on the horse, behind Sōtōko.

"Now you see why I dress like I do," said Sōtōko.

"Yes," I sighed. It was most embarrassing.

Riko and two other men came riding up to us then, dressed in lacquered-wood breastplate and epaulets. They wore no helmets, but each had a bow and a quiver of arrows slung on his back.

"Are you expecting a battle?" I asked Riko.

He shrugged. "Not really, but you never know what you'll run into in the forest. There may yet be bears foraging before they sleep for the winter, or starving villagers hoping to rob unwary travelers. Or perhaps we will be lucky and come across a deer. Better to be prepared, neh?"

I shuddered, hoping the kami of the forest would be kind and hide any deer from us.

The guardsmen opened the garden gate for us, and we rode out. I had to grasp Sōtōko's waist hard to keep from rolling off the pony's back. As we crossed the Western Road and plunged into the dark shade of the pine forest, I shivered with remembered dreams.

"It is a little cold, isn't it?" said Sōtoko. "But when the sun gets higher, it will be warmer. It is always so in the mountains."

I did not answer but watched for signs that we were on the right path. The night that Amaiko and I had fled into this forest was so long ago, and it had been so dark, and I had been so afraid, that I doubted I would recognize anything. I could only hope that Riko was right and knew the way to it himself.

Unsettling, wayward breezes blew through the pine tops. Sometimes I thought I heard laughter, or perhaps it was just the clattering of branches, one against another. As we rode deeper into the forest, dark shapes that were not clouds obscured what little sunlight filtered through the trees. Then there came deep croaking, like the caws of enormous crows, above us.

"What is that?" said Riko.

I smiled. "They are tengu."

"Tengu!" cried one of the warriors behind Riko. He took his bow off his back and fitted an arrow to the string.

"No!" I cried, but before I could explain, the warrior let the arrow fly with a mighty twang.

The tengu above us shrieked and laughed. "Awwwk! You missed! You missed, fool!" It dove down toward us. Sōtoko's horse screamed and leaped, and I tumbled off its back into the bushes.

"Ai!" Sōtoko cried as the horse bolted with her still on its back. The warriors' horses fled, too, with the men vainly trying to stop them. Only Riko managed to hold his horse somewhat in check. He looked down at me and up after Sōtoko, clearly torn.

"I am all right," I told him. "Go find her."

"I will return for you as soon as I can," said Riko, and he sped in the direction Sōtoko's horse had gone.

The cawing laughter and the shouts of the men dwindled

into the distance. I began to feel uncomfortable sprawled in the bushes, and so I stood. Or *tried* to, as my kimonos were caught in the tangle. I'm sure I ruined at least two of them getting myself unstuck.

By the time I was free of the brambles, the forest was silent, save for the wind in the pines. I felt silly just standing there, so I stepped out of the bushes and peered around. I found myself on an overgrown path, and I followed it a little ways. Just past a pair of very large pines, I stopped and gasped.

There was the kami shrine! I ran up to it, certain it had to be the same one: It looked just like a miniature house, about as high as I am tall. But it was in even worse shape than when Amaiko and I had taken refuge there. The thatched roof had fallen in on one side, and the walls leaned, and one of the sliding doors had broken off. Bits of broken pottery from old offerings crunched beneath my feet. It was a sad sight. And Dentō had been right, there was nothing impressive about the trees or view to indicate what the shrine might be dedicated to. Only a small, overgrown hummock behind it.

Still, I thought, *it should be no hard work for Riko and his men to repair the roof and those walls.*

"*Fujiwara no Mitsuko,*" said a voice cold as death behind me.

"Y-yes?" I shuddered, pulling my kimonos tighter around me, but I dared not move.

"*So. You have returned.*"

Timidly, I glanced over my shoulder. A man dressed all in gray stood there, his hair long and unbound. I should say he floated there, for when I glanced down, I saw he had no feet. A *ghost.* "Are...are you the kami of this shrine?"

The apparition nodded once, his expression hard and unfriendly. "*I am. And you are late.*"

"Forgive me," I said, turning at last and bowing deeply to

him. "I had not remembered my promise until recently. But...but I am here now, and it will be easy for my sister's husband to repair your shrine and make all well again."

"*You did not understand me,*" the ghost said. "*You are too late.*" He raised his arm and, with a sweeping gesture, brought a great gust of wind that blew my hair over my eyes and nearly blew the kimonos off my back. When the wind subsided, the little shrine was in pieces—the thatch of the roof scattered over the forest floor, the walls flat on the ground.

"What did you do that for?" I exclaimed before I could stop myself. Then I bowed again and said, "Begging your pardon, Most Ancient One, but now it will be much more difficult to repair."

"*I do not want it repaired,*" he growled. "*Look there.*" He pointed at the small hummock that rose behind where the shrine had stood. More of it was revealed now that the shrine had collapsed. On the side of the hummock, in the center of a slab of stone, was a square block of wood with an iron ring in the middle. "*Open it,*" he commanded.

"But...but I—"

"*Open it! And see what an error you have made by disrespectfully forgetting your promise to me.*"

I looked around, hoping that Riko and the others would return, but I saw no one. Not even the tengu. I walked up to the stone, grasped the iron ring, and tugged on it. It took several tugs, using all of my body's weight to pull the wood free. This revealed a dark opening in the stone. By the dim sunlight, I could discern, beyond the opening, stone steps descending into the hillside. Faintly foul air drifted out.

"It is a tomb," I whispered. "That is what the shrine was dedicated to."

"*Yes,*" said the ghost. He pointed at the opening. "*Enter, and learn who I am.*"

"But I cannot! I must not! I—"

"ENTER!"

I should have stood my ground and chanted the Lotus Sutra to drive him off. But I felt guilty for having forgotten my promise. So I gathered the skirts of my kimonos and stepped into the opening.

I had to feel my way down in the dark, and the stone wall of the stairway was cold and damp. I had descended seventeen steps when the ghost, who was right behind me, commanded, *"Stop."*

I was relieved to do so. And then a pale, greenish light filled the space in front of me. It revealed a rectangular chamber. But it was empty, save for bits of broken pottery that littered the floor.

"Once this room was filled with gold and silver," said the ghost. *"The finest of tachi swords lay here, and bronze mirrors, moon-shaped jewels, copper shields, and hardwood lances. All gone now. Stolen."*

"I am so very sorry," I said softly.

"Heh." The ghost extended his arm toward the far wall. *"They did not get it all, however. They did not find me!"* With a deep rumbling, a rectangular section of stone in the wall opened inward.

I trembled and turned to the ghost. "If you please, Most Noble Ancient Lord—"

"Yes. I know of your transgression against Lord Emma-O, Judge of the Dead. He has spoken to me. And I will see that you are taken to receive his judgment, unless you do as I bid."

So he knew. Two years before, after my brother-in-law was slain on the Western Road by the warrior monks of Heian Kyō, I had embarked on a strange journey to find my sister's grieving soul. This journey had taken me to the very court of Lord Emma-O, Judge of the Dead. I had been disguised, with ashes rubbed on my face, as a departed soul, and I had been warned not to speak. But when Emma-O said he had not seen whom

I searched for, I had whispered that that was impossible. Hearing my voice, Lord Emma-O knew I was a living person trespassing in his land, and I would have been arrested by him had not Goranu helped me escape. Ever since, I had avoided cemeteries and those realms where Lord Emma-O's demons might catch me. I had hoped staying in temples would shield me from his anger. How was I to know the kami to whom I had made a sacred promise was a powerful ghost? Naturally he would have met Lord Emma-O.

As there was nothing else I could do, I bowed my head and entered the doorway the ghost had opened.

The room beyond was bigger and dominated by a huge block of polished black stone in the center. Surrounding the black stone block were hundreds of haniwa, red-painted pottery figures depicting all manner of men, women, and animals. I had to step very carefully to make sure I knocked none of them over. The black stone block rose as high as my shoulders, so I was able to see on its top a suit of armor made solely of jade pieces bound with silver wire. But now the armor protected only bones. A magnificent mask of jade carved in the likeness of a fierce, scowling demon covered the skull.

"I was Lord Chomigoto: warrior, priest, king. As I lay dying, I asked to be buried here, where I loved to hunt, rather than on the Kinki Plain where my ancestors lay. Here I have rested for six centuries.

"Perhaps it was an error to be placed here, so far from my people. A great shrine was planned to be built outside my tomb, but it was never begun. Politics and war caused me to be forgotten. Only a village of the descendants of my most devoted followers remained here to remember, and they built the little shrine that you took refuge in."

"How very sad," I murmured. "Surely you deserved better."

"There is worse," intoned the ghost. *"A great crime was committed here. Eighty years ago, a clan of brigands moved into this*

territory. It was they who found my tomb and plundered it. The villagers tried to stop the thieves, but the robbers killed them, even women and children. Only a few escaped to scatter across the land."

"What a horrible crime," I whispered. "And you could do nothing?"

"I dwelt in the Land of the Ancestors at that time. But the wails and pleas of the dying villagers reached me in dreams, and I pleaded with Lord Emma-O to let my spirit return. He warned me it would be useless, but he granted my wish. When I arrived, however, it was too late, and I found that, as a spirit, I was powerless to avenge my people. I remembered enough of worldly wizardry to command the winds and bring nightmares, but that is all. Alone I have waited these eighty years."

"How terribly unjust," I said. "I hope my small efforts may bring you some peace."

"Peace!" boomed the ghost of Lord Chomigoto. "Do you think it is peace that I want? Oh no, I have had much time to ponder what will satisfy these years of impotent exile. And when you came to me and gave me sakaki leaves and blessings and an offer to repay a small act of kindness and protection—you, a daughter of the Nakatomi, who served the Yamato clan, who usurped the throne of my people a century after my death—I could see the karma in this and was pleased to assist you in your hour of need. That is why I have willingly suffered your forgetfulness."

"Begging your pardon, Most Ancient Noble Lord, but my clan is Fujiwara now."

"A change in name does not make a change in blood. You are of the clan who serve the Yamato. Those of your blood owe me much. Therefore, my vengeance will be combined. In accordance with your promise, you will see to it that my shrine is rebuilt—as the greatest shrine this world has seen. You will see that my tomb is restored and that which has been stolen returned

*or replaced. You will gather the remnants of my people and see
that I am properly honored once more."*

I could hardly speak for my shock. I wished I could turn
to clay and become one of the haniwa statues around me.
"But...but Chomigoto-sama...how...how can I—"

"You will take this to show you have spoken to me." A small,
square pottery tile rose into the air and fell into my hand. One
side of it had a raised symbol of a square inside two circles.
*"Now go. Do as I have commanded. If I see that you are not
doing all you can to bring this about, then I will have Lord
Emma-O send his oni-demons to drag you down to the Dungeons
of Hell."*

"Yes, Chomigoto-sama." Terrified, I gathered my kimonos
around me, bowed deeply to him, and hurried out of the chamber, through the bare room, and up the steps. Behind me, I
heard a rumbling like thunder, or the drums of Susano-wo,
Lord of Earthquakes.

I staggered out through the opening in the rock slab and
stopped to catch my breath among the debris of the small
shrine. I stood for a long time, just staring at the clay tile in my
hand. I am surprised, looking back, that I did not weep or cry.
But my karmic burden was beginning to feel so great that it no
longer seemed real—more like a tall tale told by a drunken
nobleman. Not a real life at all.

"Mitsuko! There you are!" Riko came running up to me.

In my stupefied state, I asked, "Where is your horse?"

"Spooked by those tengu. I wish your father were here to
drive them off. Have you seen Sōtōko?"

"No."

Riko swore coarsely under his breath. "I hope the others
have found her. Sōtōko!" When there came no answer, he went
on, "What are you doing over here? Why did you wander from
where I had left you? Oh. Was this your shrine?"

"Yes."

"Not much left, I see. Looks like it was a simple one, though. Should be easy enough to replace. Sōtōko!" There was still no answer, and I suspect he continued talking to me to hide his growing fear. "Yes. Wood, paper, some thatch. We can gather all of these. Have it done in a day or two. Sōtōko!"

I shook my head. "Forgive me, Riko, but it is no longer so simple. It will have to be a bigger shrine."

"What?" He frowned at me and then noticed the opening in the hill behind me. His face turned pale. "Is...is that a tomb?"

"Yes. I have met the kami of the shrine. It is the ghost of an ancient Kofun priest-king. He is buried there."

His eyes widened. "Sōtōko didn't go in there, did she?"

"No. I did. The tomb has been plundered, and the villagers who served the shrine were murdered long ago. The kami wants me to restore his tomb, and build a great shrine to him, and gather what is left of his people so that he may be honored once more."

"Did you ask the kami where Sōtōko was?"

Truly, it seems people never listen to me. "I did not have the chance. He gave me this to prove that I had spoken with him." I handed Riko the clay tile.

He stared down at it, and, if anything, his face turned even more pale.

As he did not speak, I babbled on. "We must talk to your father, Lord Tsubushima, and ask his help. I do not know what more I can do. Surely your father knows this land and can give advice."

"I recognize this symbol," said Riko, still gazing at the tile. "I saw it on many things at my great-uncle's house. I remember stories I heard at his knee, about how our clan's ancestors came upon an abandoned tomb, and took its treasure, and wiped out the tribe of barbarians who guarded it. That, I was told, was how our clan acquired wealth and rose to greatness."

I stared at him. "So it was *your* ancestors who killed the villagers?"

Riko stared at the tomb opening, his face full of dread. "It would seem so. If this kami is truly the spirit of the lord-king of the tomb, you can expect no help from my father. He has ambitions that our family will join the ranks of the great nobility of Heian Kyō someday. He will do nothing that might reveal such a shameful event in our family's past."

The sky seemed to have grown darker, and contrary breezes tugged at my hair and clothes. "Then I am lost," I whispered. Riko apparently did not hear me, or chose not to.

"If I had known this tomb was here, I would never have brought you into this forest. You do not think," Riko said, his voice wavering, "that those tengu were sent by the kami—that he is taking vengeance by harming Sōtōko, do you?"

"Tengu do not kill," I said wearily. "They just like to play tricks. The kami did not mention my sister at all."

"Riko!" It sounded like Sōtōko, calling from some distance away.

He looked up sharply from the tile. "Sōtōko! Stay where you are! I'll be right there!" He dropped the clay tile and took off at a run toward the voice.

I bent down and picked up the clay tile and slipped it into my sleeve. My heart numb, I thought, *Surely, there can be no one else in the world as wretched as I am now.*

> Is this how an ant
> feels when the stone he lifts in
> his jaws crushes him?

Awareness

Chirping in the fog.
Is it a bird or a frog?
Crunch. Oh. A cricket.

$\mathcal{I}$ DO NOT KNOW how long I stood, unmoving, in the clearing. I understood now how one could wish one's soul to flee the body when a burden becomes too great to bear.

The rattling clatter of beaks and the fluttering of wings intruded on my thoughts. Five tengu, wearing the shapes of enormous ravens, landed in the clearing in front of me.

"Riko! Riko!" one of them said in perfect imitation of Sōtōko's voice. The other tengu laughed.

A flash of anger cut through my sorrows as a lightning bolt will, for a moment, rend dark clouds. "Stop that!" I said to the tengu.

"Ooooh, look what we have here!"

"It's Prince Goranu's little noble girl."

"The one who drove him mad."

"The one who made him want to be a Buddhist so he could be reborn a mortal."

"Stop it!" I said again. "Did Lord Chomigoto send you here to make me even more miserable?"

"Nobody sends *us* anywhere!"

"Though we're very open to suggestion."

"Besides, you deserve to be miserable after what you've done to Prince Goranu."

"But I have done nothing to him," I said, my hands clenched into fists at my sides. "He chose to—"

"Nothing? Why, you impudent mortal, Goranu has hidden himself away from the rest of us reading a sutra you gave to him. His fingers and mouth are nearly burnt black."

Poor Goranu. If only I could have convinced him that I was an unworthy reason for his seeking the Heavenward Path. If only I could speak to him again, perhaps I could distract him with my misery. But how?

Then in the wild mood that sometimes comes with despair, I turned to the closest tengu and said, "You are lying."

The tengu jumped back, aghast. "What?"

"What!" cried the other tengu, beaks agape.

"We tengu never lie!"

"Unless we feel like it."

"I know you are lying," I persisted. "Because you want me to feel bad. You are just teasing me."

"Of course we are teasing. That is what tengu do."

"But that doesn't mean we're lying."

"Prince Goranu is in terrible pain right this very moment."

"And it is all your fault."

I crossed my arms on my chest. "I do not believe you. I think that even now Goranu is watching us, ready to laugh at me for believing your lies."

The tengu all stepped back, clacking their beaks and fluffing their feathers.

"How dare she!"

"The impudence!"

"What a callous little thing she is!"

"She stands there and calls us liars while her lover is dying."

"If you want me to believe you," I said, "you will have to prove it."

The lead tengu took a hop toward me. "I am Kuroihane, Leaflet Tengu and second only to Prince Goranu himself. Your accusations do me great dishonor. You want proof? Very well. We will show you."

"No, no," I said. "I know all about your illusions. They will not prove anything. You must take me to Prince Goranu so that I may see with my own eyes and hear with my own ears whether you are telling the truth or not."

The tengu looked at one another.

"Demanding little creature!"

"Do you even have a heart capable of pity?"

The one called Kuroihane glared at me through his crow black eyes. "Yes. We will take you to our Prince Goranu and let you see for yourself the horrible thing you have done."

I waited as they produced from somewhere a net made of rope and bade me step into it. I did so, remembering the night two years before when Amaiko and I were carried in such a net to the village of the tengu. It felt as though it had been a lifetime ago.

I crouched down and grasped the rough net as the tengu leaped into the air. They were not gentle with me, and the net lurched and swayed and bashed into treetops as we rose above the forest. From the height, I could see Riko and Sōtōko in another clearing not far away. "Good-bye!" I called out to them. They looked up and pointed.

"Mitsuko!" Sōtōko cried.

"Do not worry about me!" I shouted back at her. "I shall be all right. Good-bye!" I do not know how much they heard, the tengu were carrying me away so fast. I wished I could thank Sōtōko and Riko for their hospitality and hoped someday I would have the chance.

We flew high above the forested slopes. The temples and monastery sitting on the flanks of Mount Hiei looked almost peaceful from that height and distance, the morning sun glinting off of their tiled roofs, smoke drifting up lazily from cooking fires. We swung away from the sight of Mount Hiei and again before me was the tall cliff with its long, narrow shadow running down it—a wind-carved hole in the rock wall, just wide and tall enough for us all to fly through. It took only a moment for us to pass through the dark cleft to the other side, where a deep valley with a little village in it opened up below us. These tengu were not disposed to treating me kindly, however, so instead of letting me down gently, I was bump-bump-bumped along the ground until we stopped.

I stood, rubbing those places where I surely was bruised. "That was unkind," I said, glaring at Kuroihane.

"Unkind? Us? Let us see who is most unkind. There." He pointed with the tip of his wing toward the nearest thatched hut. "There is where poor Goranu lies, breathing his last with burning prayers."

I brushed the dirt off my kimonos. "I will see him for myself before I will believe you."

"Go and look then, heartless creature. We will not stop you."

I tossed my head as if I did not care and walked straight to the hut. At the curtained doorway, I heard a strange croaking from inside, and I hesitated, my hand on the curtain. They were sacred words, but the pain in that voice! My courage nearly failed me. The tengu who had carried me here were right behind me, preventing me from turning back.

"Go on."

"What are you afraid of?"

"Afraid of the truth?"

"Afraid of seeing what you have done?"

I growled at them, "I have met the Dragon King, Ryujin, and I have met your Esteemed Ancestor Susano-wo, and I have met the Lord of Death himself. What have I to fear?" I pulled open the curtain and stepped up into the hut.

There was a smell of burnt hair and feathers in the air. Goranu lay sprawled, in mostly human form, in a corner of the tiny hut. He clasped the sutra copy I had made against his chest. It was he making the croaking noise, trying to say the Lotus Sutra. All my feelings of self-pity melted away as I crept closer to him.

Ai! He was a horrible sight. His lips were blackened, cracked, and bleeding, as were his fingers. His half-shut eyes were red and oozing. What feathers remained on his body were scorched.

"Oh, Goranu," I whispered, "do you understand now why I would not teach you the sutras?"

He did not seem to hear me or know I was there. Gently, I took the scroll out of his hands and laid it aside. At this, Goranu stopped his croaking chant. "Awk, what thief is it who steals the holy words?" he rasped.

"It is me, your friend, Mitsuko," I said, taking his hands carefully in mine. "Please do not die, Goranu."

"I . . . must continue," he whispered. "I must . . . be reborn . . . a mortal."

"No, that is unworthy," I said, fighting back tears. "One learns the sutras to gain enlightenment, to escape the Wheel of Rebirth, not so that you may choose what creature to be in the next life."

He reached up with one burnt and blistered finger and touched my cheek. "I want . . . to be . . . with you." He laid his head upon my lap.

"I am here," I whispered, gently taking his hands in mine.

And then I could no longer stop myself, and I wept. Because I held his hands, I could not cover my eyes with my sleeves to soak up my tears, which flowed freely onto Goranu's fingers and dripped onto his face. I do not know how long I knelt beside him that way.

After a while, however, I heard the other tengu behind me, saying, "Well, will you look at that!"

"Amazing!"

"I didn't know she could do that."

"Maybe we should have brought her sooner."

I blinked my eyes and peered around, trying to see what they were talking about. Then I looked down. Goranu's hands were healing where my tears had dripped onto them. I wiped my eyes with the edge of my sleeve and dabbed Goranu's lips and eyelids with it. These, too, began to heal. And I remembered a time two years ago when Goranu had burnt his feet while rescuing me from the Temple of Kiyomizudera. I had wept over his feet and bandaged them, and then was amazed at how quickly he had healed.

"Tears of maidenly pity," said Kuroihane behind me. "No wonder. Such tenderness has great healing power for us."

"Why?" I turned and looked at the raven-headed creature. "Why should my tears matter?"

"Heh. No doubt it was a jest on the part of our Esteemed Ancestor. What human maiden would weep for a tengu, after all?"

"I do."

Kuroihane closed his eyes and bowed. "Clearly our Prince Goranu was right, and you are a creature extraordinary for your kind."

Goranu sighed deeply, and I looked down. He had closed his eyes, and his hands fell limp from mine.

"Ai, no!" I cried, fearing the worst.

Kuroihane pried open one of Goranu's eyelids, then turned

to me with a sardonic look. "Silly girl. He is only sleeping. He has been up for many hours reading your stupid sutra, after all." The tengu took Goranu from my lap and laid him out on the floor, covering him with a cloak. "Thank you for helping him," said Kuroihane at last. "Now get out before you cause more trouble."

"Will he . . . be all right?"

"If he can forget about you and your foolish religion, he will be fine. Now go."

Stung by the tengu's rudeness, I said nothing, and hurried out of the hut.

Though it was bright late morning, I saw no other tengu in the village. It appeared deserted, so I presumed all the rest were sleeping. I walked down the path through the center of the village, wondering what to do. Even though I had saved Goranu, the other tengu were not very grateful. I doubted that I could ask any of them for help with my debts to Lord Chomigoto. I was so tired and hungry that I began to consider searching for the nearest graveyard and simply giving myself up to Lord Emma-O. It would be pleasing to be free of this world and its weighty problems, even if it meant dwelling in the Hell of Headlong Falling for a time, until my soul could move on.

"Help?" I heard from not far away. "Please let me out of here." It was not a tengu voice—in fact, it sounded familiar. I looked around and saw a tall tree behind one of the huts. There seemed to be something like a large cage hanging from one of its branches.

Lifting the hems of my kimonos, I ran around the hut and saw there was a girl in the cage. She turned her head to look at me.

"Suzume?" I cried in astonishment.

"Oh, Great Lady Little Mountain Puddle! I knew you would find me. Please get me out of this." She shook the bars of her bamboo cage.

I walked up, but the cage was too high, just out of my reach. "I cannot. Oh, Suzume, how did you get here?"

"I will tell you everything, but please get me out!"

I looked around and saw an old man, or a tengu in old-man form, emerge from the nearest hut. "Venerable Sir," I said to him, in what I hoped were fine and imperious tones like my mama once used. "Would you please be so helpful as to release my servant from this cage?"

"Who, her?" From the old man's cackle, I could tell he was a tengu. "She is yours, is she? How very interesting. Perhaps you would like to know why she is caged in a tengu village, eh?"

"I will listen avidly to all you say, as soon as you release her!"

"Nope. Can't do that."

"But I am a Fujiwara, and I demand it!"

This sent the tengu in old-man form into howling laughter, and his body shook so with his *ha-ha*s and *hee-hee*s that he had to sit down on the ground. I wanted to pummel him. But that would have been entirely unsuitable, so I pulled my hair instead. "I do not see what is amusing. Release her at once!"

This only made the old-man tengu hoot louder, and he grabbed his knees to his chest and rolled on the ground as he laughed.

"Forgive my observation if it is rude," said Suzume, "but I do not think your method is working. Ah, here comes a bird-man. Maybe you can make him laugh, too."

I turned before I could snap at Suzume and saw a tengu in the strange half-man–half-raven form, with both wings and arms, and a beak. "Can't help disrupting things wherever you go, can you?" he said to me.

So it was Kuroihane. "I meant no disruption," I said. "But this is my servant who is caged here, and I want her released."

Kuroihane spat out a growled caw at me and kicked the old

man on the ground. "You. Get up. Prince Goranu says you can let the mortal girl go."

"He does?" asked the old-man tengu, sitting up. "Well, that's different then." He stood and clambered up the tree as easily as a monkey. He crawled out onto the branch holding the cage and released the catch or knot holding it there. The cage crashed to the ground with a thud.

I ran up to it. "Suzume! Are you all right?"

"I think so." She stood, rubbing her elbows and knees, though they had been padded by her layers of kimonos. "My brother and I used to climb and jump out of trees all the time."

I tried to imagine a life where one could do such things, and it seemed very strange. My sisters and I had been taught to admire trees and write poems about them, not climb them.

The old tengu dropped down from the branch and untied the knot of the cage door. Suzume pushed it open and stumbled out.

"Now," I said to the old-man tengu, "why was she in a cage?"

But it was Kuroihane who answered. "You might be interested to know that after Prince Goranu flew you to your sister's house and came back here with that cursed scroll, he felt someone else summoning him. He was so eager to read those ridiculous sutras, he sent us to see who had the impertinence to call him, since he knew it wasn't you. Well, we found this little creature in some nobleman's yard in Heian Kyō, with one of Goranu's feathers, saying Goranu's name. So we brought her here and caged her up until Goranu could decide what to do with her."

"Is this true?" I asked Suzume.

She nodded, hanging her head. "I did not know what to do when I saw you flying away on the tengu's back. Really, you place quite a burden on your servants, you know? I was afraid your father would blame me for your running away and beat me or throw my family back onto the street. So I found the feather in the garden, and I did just what you did. And a tengu came and carried me away. I hoped I could find you and talk you into coming back before anyone noticed we were gone. But it is too late now. Now they will find us both missing and truly wonder." She wiped away a tear with her sleeve.

"Poor Suzume," I said, hoping to calm her. "I did not realize what effect my actions might have on you. I do not think my father would have beaten you or sent you and your family away." Given how angry and upset he had been when he demanded that I marry Prince Komakai, I truly did not know *what* he might have done. "But you should not have used the feather to call the tengu."

"I am beginning to see that now," Suzume said.

I had a frightening thought and turned to Kuroihane. "What would you have done with her if Goranu had died?"

"Oh, I don't know." He tilted his head to regard her as a bird does a possibly edible worm. "Probably something quite entertaining . . . though rather unpleasant for her. A pity you have robbed us of such a game. Oh well. Try not to cause any more trouble, either of you, or we'll fly you to the top of Morning Sun Cliff and drop you there." With that, he turned to the old-man tengu and said, "You, come with me." The two tengu walked away through the village without another look at us.

"So," said Suzume, "this is where your demon friend lives. Such nasty creatures they are."

"Goranu is . . . not like them," I said, although in some ways he was.

Suddenly, Suzume flung herself prostrate on the ground at my feet. "Forgive me, Lady Mistress!" she cried.

"Oh, stop it," I said, sighing.

"But I have caused you trouble by behaving foolishly." She

tilted her head to regard me through strands of her hair. "Isn't this what I'm supposed to do?"

"Oh, I do not know. It does not matter now what you are supposed to do. We are not in the Palace or my father's house."

Suzume stood and straightened her kimonos...incorrectly, I noted. "I'm sorry, then. There is so much that I haven't learned yet. Sometimes I think life was easier as a rice cake girl."

"I am sure you are right," I said.

"Will you forgive me if I tell you something else?"

"I am sure I will."

"You look terrible."

Such a comment coming from her almost made me laugh. "I what?"

"No, really. You look the way you did two years ago when your house burned down and you had to come stay with me."

"That bad?" My hand strayed to my hair, which, of course, was all tousled. I had not thought about it, but my kimonos had been torn by the brambles in the forest, and my face was doubtless pale from shock, and my eyes red from weeping. "Yes, I suppose you are right."

"Here." Suzume reached into the bottom of her deep sleeve. "I have some rice cakes left. I brought them thinking I might need to bribe the tengu." She handed me one.

It had been crushed out of whatever shape it had been first molded into, but there were bits of seaweed and poppy seeds on it, and the handful of rice tasted wonderful. "Thank you," I said, covering my mouth because it was still full of rice.

Suzume laughed, and I almost did, too. "If you please, Great Lady," she said, "let us get out of this dreary village and find a pleasanter place to eat the rest of these."

I nodded, and we walked away from the huts. We followed a path that led up the hillside of the valley, hoping for an enjoyable view. But the clouds drifted lower and lower until we couldn't see the tengu village at all.

We finally stopped at a rock outcropping that overlooked a pool of water. On a sunny day, this place might have been lovely, but the mist was now so heavy around us that it felt eerie, as though we were cut off from the rest of the world.

As we ate our rice cakes, I told Suzume all about the shrine and Lord Chomigoto and the things he demanded of me. Mama used to say that confiding in one's servants was a mistake, for they remember everything you say and might gossip or do even more harmful things with it later. But Suzume was different. She had been my friend first. And there was no one else around to trust. So I blurted out the whole story to her.

When I had finished, she said, "So...why didn't you bargain with the ghost?"

"What? Bargain with the ghost of a warrior priest-king?"

"Why not? You know, if you can't do all those things he asked for, you should have talked him down to just fixing the shrine. That's what my papa would have done. When he buys rice from the farmers, they always try to ask a high price. He talks them down to what is reasonable, which is what they expect him to do, so no one is upset. It's just a game, he says, and the only person hurt is the stupid merchant who won't bargain."

I am sure my mouth hung open.

"Ooops," Suzume said, eyes suddenly wide. "I didn't mean to say *you* were stupid, Great Lady."

"No, of course you did not," I said, wondering if she had.

"It's just—you don't even know if the ghost was telling the truth. How do you know he was all those things he claimed to be?"

"I saw his tomb. What is left was magnificent, things only a king would have. And Riko confirmed his story."

"So these are the things we know." Suzume held up her fingers. "One, he was probably a king. Two, he had a shrine that a nearby village served. Three, Lord Tsubushima's clan destroyed that village and plundered the tomb."

"Yes," I said. "So how could the ghost be lying?"

"Well, how do you know Chomigoto is such a friend of Lord Emma-O that he can make the Lord of Death punish you if you don't do as he asked? You say that all Chomigoto-sama can command are the winds and dreams."

I paused, uncertain. "But...well...it would seem natural that he is acquainted with Lord Emma-O."

"So is almost any ghost, since most people pass through Emma-O's court, if the stories are true," said Suzume. "That doesn't mean your ghost is telling the truth. Maybe Lord Emma-O banished him to our world for some other reason. And here he finds a young noble girl he can frighten into improving his lot in life—well, afterlife. Maybe his tomb is far away and forgotten because he was a bad king. Or he ruled only for a very short time and there is no reason to remember or worship him."

I was so shaken, I could hardly speak. "But...I did make a sacred promise to him. And my sister and I were safely sheltered, and the tengu did come for us."

"I'm not sure a visit from the tengu could be called 'help,' " Suzume said, glaring back toward the village.

"Anyway, I promised; so I must do something, neh?"

"How do you know it was Chomigoto who sent the tengu? I thought tengu lived in that forest, or went there often. Perhaps he did nothing and is just taking advantage of your trust to get you to do things for him."

I could not answer. Truly, it was amazing how suspicious Suzume was, and yet, if she was right, what a fool I had been! I could ask the tengu. I could ask Goranu, now that he was healing. He was there that night, after all. I would not be asking him to do anything for me, so I would not be demanding much. I resolved to do so.

We sat in silence for a long while, eating the last crumbs of the rice cakes. The mist had quite closed in now, and I could see nothing beyond the pool and the rocks on the other side. It seemed appropriate to be so isolated from the rest of the world. Suzume's words had so turned my thoughts upside down that I no longer knew what sort of world I lived in.

> *One sees a mirror,*
> *one sees a pool of water;*
> *all is illusion.*

I was startled by the sound of something scuttling in the tall grass nearby.

Suzume leaned close and whispered in my ear, "Look, down there by the water's edge."

I did and saw a pair of thin little yellow-green arms and hands dipping a pinecone into the water and washing it. "How charming," I whispered back. "I have never seen a wild monkey so close."

"That's not a monkey. Look at it more closely."

The creature moved into the water a bit, and I saw it had a turtle's back. Its hands were webbed like a frog's, and its head was like a monkey's except for a depression in the crown.

"It's a kappa," said Suzume. "They say that kappa like to drown people, especially little boys who are bad. And they drink blood. But they also say it can be good luck to catch one, for kappa have much knowledge and magic. If the water on top of its head spills off, it will become weak. So if you catch it and threaten to turn it upside-down, you can make it promise you all sorts of things in exchange for letting it go."

I turned and frowned at her. "What a terrible thing to do to such a creature."

"Oh, don't be that way. Kappa are nasty beasts, and besides, we wouldn't really hurt it, just threaten to. You need help right now, don't you? Come on, let's see if we can grab it."

She slid off the rock and crept toward the animal before I could grab her sleeve to stop her. I was sure I could not move fast enough in my kimonos to catch such a creature, even if I wanted to, which I did not.

The kappa heard Suzume approaching and stood up straight in alarm. It chittered a moment, dropped the pinecone, and ran off up the hillside under the grass and ferns. Its gait was awkward as it tried to keep its head upright. Suzume ran determinedly after it, and soon she disappeared into the mist.

"Suzume!" I jumped off the rock and ran after her. "Suzume!" Mama once said the Good People must always look after their servants, but I felt very annoyed. What can one do if the servant insists on behaving foolishly? Nonetheless, I followed her, trying to run uphill in my bulky kimonos and wooden sandals, as the mist drifted close around me, clinging to my trailing sleeves.

Individuality

The moon sits on a
puddle; until I touch it—
then it is shattered!

I RAN UNTIL I was nearly out of breath. Then, dimly through the mist, I saw Suzume up ahead of me, sitting on a low stone. I staggered up and plopped down on the rock beside her, unable to speak for my gasping.

"I couldn't catch it," Suzume said, despondent.

"And now," I said, when I could speak again, "we are lost." The fog was so thick that we could see no more than the immediate ground around us.

"Not really," Suzume said. "We know we have to go downhill. Eventually, we'd reach the valley. Then we'd turn to our right and walk until we reached the tengu village. It's simple. I had to learn a good sense of direction in the streets of Heian Kyō."

I, however, had wandered on stranger paths than Suzume

would ever see, and I was not convinced that proceeding back the way we came would return us to where we started.

"Should we start back now, Great Lady Puddle?"

"Allow me to catch my breath more, if you please." I wasn't sure I liked her calling me that, but I did not know what else to suggest. We sat together in silence as the fog crept closer and our hair and clothes grew damp.

As I was beginning to consider standing up for the long walk back, I saw red-orange light flickering in the gloom ahead of us, farther up the mountainside. At first I thought it might be torchlight, but as it approached, it seemed too low to the ground.

Suzume noticed it, too. "What is that?"

"I do not know. Do kappa carry torches?"

"Not that I have heard."

And then it came out of the mist. A small creature, looking somewhat like a dog, except that it had hooves like a deer, and short straight horns. But most amazing of all were the flames that flickered about its shoulders and hindquarters.

Suzume leaned close to me. "What is it? Is it dangerous?"

"I have seen it in paintings. Ah, now I remember. It is a kirin."

"I have not heard tales about kirin."

"I do not remember anything about them, except that they are messengers of a sort. I do not think they are dangerous." In truth, I was not sure at all, but I did not want to frighten Suzume or myself.

The kirin stopped a short distance away and said, in a high, flutelike voice, "Greetings. You are here, no doubt, to consult with Kai-Lung, Keeper of Knowledge, the Wisest of the Wise."

Suzume and I looked at one another. "What does it mean?" she asked me. "What sort of name is Kai-Lung?"

"It sounds Chinese to me," I replied. "My father speaks and reads that language, and I have heard him tell of great scholars who used to come from Chang'an to teach in Heian Kyō. Maybe this Kai-Lung is one such traveling philosopher who has taken hermitage in the mountains."

"Yes," said the kirin, with what seemed to be a smile. "Kai-Lung has traveled here from across the Western Sea."

"Well, maybe we should talk to him," said Suzume. "We are in need of wisdom. Maybe he can tell us what to do about your ghost-king."

I was worried about disturbing the meditations of a philosopher, but the words of the kirin implied that he expected visitors. "Perhaps you are right."

Suzume boldly stood and bowed to the kirin. "This is Great Lady Fujiwara no Mitsuko, and she wishes to have audience with the wise Kai-Lung. Please do us the honor of taking us to him at once."

Well, she was learning—although servants properly should not include themselves in any business. They are best if they are invisible, Mama always used to say.

The kirin tittered and then coughed. "As you wish. Please do me the honor of following me." It turned around and tripped daintily along the mountain path.

We followed, but with considerably more difficulty. At one point we had to climb over some steep rocks, and in another place we skittered over slippery rocks that were flat as plates. At last, Suzume and I stood in a patch of bare dirt surrounded by dark, shadowed mist, as if some cliff or other feature loomed very close all around us.

"Kai-Lung will speak with you shortly," said the kirin, and disappeared. I could not tell if it was by magic or just the mist.

Suzume and I stood close together for some time. I confess I was frightened by the gloom and the occasional, muffled sound of rock sliding against rock. I wondered what the philosopher could be doing. Building a wall? I think Suzume was frightened, too, from the way she clung to my sleeve.

Suddenly, there came a rumble like continuous thunder, and I wondered if rocks were going to come raining down on us. Suzume and I held on to each other, as we could see nowhere to run.

A huge boulder emerged from the mist—no! It was an enormous bewhiskered snout, followed by a reptilian head with eyes as big as my face and horns as long as I am tall.

"A dragon!" Suzume screamed, and she fell to her knees. I stood as if I had been frozen into ice. I had seen dragons before, but only from a distance. They had been swimming in the waves behind King Ryujin when I met him on the beach of Enoshima. And, as Riko had so well remembered, in the sky above Lord Tsubushima's castle. But I had never been so close to a dragon as this. I was sure it could devour me in one bite if it wished. We looked all around and saw that the dragon's long, scaly body surrounded us, high as a wall, impassable. I realized with horror that some of the rocks we walked over to reach this place must have been the scales of the dragon itself.

"I am the one who is called Kai-Lung," said the dragon in a voice like the rumble of an earthquake. "Who wishes to speak with me?"

I looked at Suzume, but she appeared no longer interested in doing formal announcements. I bowed very low to the dragon and said, "I...I...do. I am Fujiwara no Mitsuko." Then, in a flash of inspiration, I added, "I send greetings to your king, Ryujin-sama."

"Ah," said Kai-Lung. "You know of the Dragon King of the Sea?"

"I...had the honor of meeting him two years ago. He did me a kindness then, which I have not forgotten."

"You were honored, indeed," said Kai-Lung. "What is your question?"

"My...question?"

"You have come to me for wisdom, have you not? Please

do not be tiresome. I allow one question to any mortal brave
and fortunate enough to find me. What is your question?"

I bowed my head, wishing I had more time to give thought
to how I would ask for help. "Oh Great Kai-Lung—" I began.

"That is redundant," the dragon muttered.

I pressed on. "I made a promise to one who now demands
of me more than I promised. This one threatens to harm me if
I do not do all he asks; yet what he asks is not in my power,
nor can I find anyone who has such power to help me."

"And your question is?" asked the dragon.

I flailed the air around me with my arms, feeling helpless.
"What do I do now? You see, the one I made the promise to is
the ghost of an ancient king and—"

"Enough!" The dragon lowered his head to the ground. "I
will now contemplate your question. Do not speak to me again
until I have answered it." Kai-Lung then closed his eyes and
became very still.

As I waited, I became more perplexed. How could even a
wise creature such as this understand my situation without
knowing the details? Suzume and I huddled together, and I
wondered if we would be forced to wait for hours, days, or
longer.

"What will your question be, when it is your turn?" I asked
her, my head resting on her shoulder.

"I think I will ask him how we get home."

"You are more practical than I am."

"That is what servants are for, neh?"

We did not, as it happens, have to wait very long before
Kai-Lung again raised his massive head and opened his eyes. "I
have your answer," he rumbled.

Suzume and I stood up, and I said, "I am ready to hear it."

"You," Kai-Lung intoned, "have been foolish. Therefore, go.
And be foolish no more."

I waited for further explication, but there came none.

"Is that all?" asked Suzume. "We have come all this way just to hear that? Why, you could have said that to almost any mortal, for almost any question!"

"Yes," said Kai-Lung, with a sardonic smile. "I could. And that, I assume, was *your* question, and I have answered it."

"This isn't fair!" said Suzume. "You must give the Great Lady more of an answer than that, and that wasn't my question!"

"Suzume—" I said, trying to calm her.

"*What!*" roared Kai-Lung, raising his head to tower over us. "You dare to say my answers are unacceptable?" His eyes began to glow red, and steam rushed from his nostrils.

The earth shook beneath my feet, and I could hear rocks tumbling from cliffs nearby. I grabbed Suzume and covered her mouth. "Please forgive us, Great Kai-Lung. We meant no disrespect! We will leave your presence and trouble you no more." I pulled Suzume with me as I ran out of the clearing.

Behind us, the mountain continued to thunder with Kai-Lung's roars, shaking the ground beneath us. We scrambled down the hillside, sometimes tumbling and rolling a little ways before we regained our footing. I am sure my outer kimono was a complete ruin. Down and down we ran, and I did not know if the path my feet had found was the right one or not. Down and down, until we were below the mist, and I heard someone call, "There they are!"

I tripped again and tumbled until I came to a stop, breathless, at the feet of the tengu Kuroihane.

"You see, Prince Goranu? These mortals get into trouble no matter what you tell them. We should never have brought them here."

I looked up to see Goranu in his young-man-with-a-long-nose form staring down at me. His gaze might have been fond, but he did not look happy. "I am beginning to think you are right, Kuroihane."

"It wasn't our fault!" said Suzume, running up behind me.

I stood, feeling quite embarrassed, and dusted myself off. "Please forgive us," I said with a bow. "We did not mean to upset the dragon. I did not even know he was there until Suzume decided to chase a kappa. And then a kirin asked us if we wanted to see Kai-Lung and, thinking he was just a hermit scholar, I said yes. And then the dragon asked me for a question, then gave me a useless answer, and when we told him so, he became angry, and we ran away."

Goranu tilted his head and regarded me with a strange little smile. "I see I have been a bad influence on you, Little Puddle. You have become nearly as silly as a tengu."

"But it is all true!" I said, exasperated.

"That," said Goranu, "is what makes it so silly. Will you come aside and talk with me, in private?"

"Of course." As we began to walk away, Suzume started to follow us.

Goranu turned and said to her, "In private does not mean servants can come along."

Suzume backed up a step, eyes wide. "But the Great Lady must have a chaperone nearby."

"The so-called Great Lady and I have done well enough without one for two years," grumbled Goranu. "We don't need any eavesdropping gossips now. You just wait here until we return."

Suzume looked back and forth, from me to Goranu. "But..."

"Please, Suzume, do as he says," I told her.

"Hmpf." Suzume flounced her kimonos and, tossing her head, turned to walk away. Over her shoulder, she said to me, "You never warned me that tengu were so rude."

"Just be glad you are not a monk," Goranu shouted after her. "*Then* you would see tengu rudeness."

"Poor thing," I said as Goranu and I walked. "She wants to

learn how to be a proper servant, and I am not a very good teacher."

"Indeed," said Goranu. He was staring at the ground, and his arms were hidden within his jacket sleeves.

I was uncertain what he meant. "I am glad to see you are better. Did you have a good rest?" I asked, hoping to draw him out more.

"Good? No, I would not call it good." He did not say more, and I became frustrated with his reticence.

"This fog, it is so dreary," I said at last. "It certainly dampens one's spirits, as well as one's sleeves."

"Well, there is no need for the Great Lady to suffer so," said Goranu, and he waved his hands about. Suddenly, we were standing before a charming little pavilion that overlooked a gorge filled with ribbonlike waterfalls. The sun shone through a blue sky, and birds sang sweetly in the nearby pine trees.

I nearly danced into the pavilion. "Why, this is wonderful, Goranu! Beautiful!"

"Oh, don't get so excited," said Goranu, slumping against a support pillar of the pavilion. "It is just an illusion, after all."

My patience was tried too far for me to remain polite. "Whatever is the matter with you?"

Goranu sat down on the ground, his back against the pillar. He gazed upon me with an expression I could not read. "You truly do not understand, do you?"

"I regret that my troubles lately may have made me blind."

"Indeed, I think they have. Or perhaps you have always been so. It may be one of your most attractive features."

I sighed noisily and sat down on the pavilion floor, some distance from him.

Goranu stared out at the waterfalls. "After you took the sutra scroll from me, while I was sleeping, I had a dream."

"Do tengu dream, then?"

"We are not as unlike you mortals as you think. In my dream, I was visited by three shining personages who came down from the clouds to speak to me."

"Truly? But this is very good news, Goranu! Those personages must surely have been bosatsu: those souls who have denied themselves entrance to nirvana so that they may help other souls along the Heavenward Path."

"I know that," snapped Goranu. "Do you want to hear the dream or not?"

"Your pardon," I said. "Please, go on."

"The first one was a skinny fellow. Looked like he had been starving awhile. He came down a mountain and smiled at me and said I shouldn't be upset at failing to achieve enlightenment."

"Ah! That would be Sakyamuni," I said. "He tried fasting to find the path, but it failed. He found another way to enlightenment later."

"He told me that, in a previous life, I was a monk who had fallen away from proper behavior. That was why I was reborn a tengu. Can you imagine? Me...a monk! What greater insult could he give me?" Goranu crossed his arms on his chest and scowled at the waterfalls.

"I can imagine it," I said, but too softly for him to hear.

"Then he left, and another spirit arrived, riding a lion and holding a scroll in one hand and a sword in the other. A plump, pretty fellow like some of your noblemen at Court."

"Ah, that would be Monju-bosatsu. He is a spirit of great learning and knowledge."

"Yes, well, this fellow said that I was being a fool and that my feet would never find the Path, because I was heading the wrong direction and my motives were not pure. Can you imagine that? A nobleman saying *my* thoughts weren't pure!"

"Yes," I whispered. "I can imagine it."

"The third spirit," Goranu went on, "was the biggest show-off of all. He came in sitting on a lotus blossom, on top of a four-headed white elephant."

"Fugen-bosatsu," I said, nodding. "He governs long life and compassion."

"Whatever. He, at least, spoke to me with a bit of kindness and told me all was not lost. He said there was a way to achieve what I wished without killing myself over it. Then he left before telling me what that way might be!"

"Such is the nature of dreams," I said. "But what is it you wish?"

He stared at me intently. "I have told you what I wish. Two years ago, remember?"

I looked down at the floor and saw the wood grain waver. "Yes, I believe I do remember."

"I told you I wanted to marry you. But...it is forbidden in tengu culture for us to marry mortals."

I felt as unsettled as the waters beneath the cataracts in the gorge. The thought of marriage to Goranu was bizarre, and yet...pleasant. But many people think of tengu as demons. I said softly, "In mortal custom, also, it would be forbidden."

"So. In our present lives it cannot be. But I was hoping if I could die and be reborn a mortal, there might be a chance. Our lives are so entwined that surely we will meet again in another, future life, I thought. Alas, the bosatsu say that my hopes are foolish. I am just a silly tengu after all."

I did not know what to say, so I did not respond.

His gaze upon me changed. "It is not impossible, not un-known, that a tengu might...love a mortal. Even create a child by one..." He swiftly looked away. "But that would shame you. And I could not do that."

I pulled my kimonos tighter around me, as if to hold in my feelings, as a gardener will build a rock wall beside a spring stream to keep the rising waters from invading the flower beds.

Part of me wanted Goranu to stop speaking of such forbidden things. Another part wanted to hear of nothing else.

"Besides," Goranu continued in a forced hearty tone, "it is intended that you marry an eleven-year-old cousin of the Emperor. Surely the affections of a tengu pale in comparison."

I slapped the floor of the pavilion with the heel of my hand. "Stop that! I will not marry Prince Komakai! Not if...I can avoid it." I ran my fingers over the wood grain of the floor planks. How real it seemed for an illusion. "Besides," I went on, "if I disappoint Lord Chomigoto, I will be going to the Hall of Death very soon anyway."

"Lord Chomigoto!" said Goranu, sitting up suddenly. "Old Blowhard the ghost? What has he to do with you?"

"Do you not remember? Wasn't it he who sent you to the shrine in the forest where you found Amaiko and me?"

Goranu scratched his chin. "Let me see. I don't remember talking to him that night. I do remember something in the wind, but nobody sent us to the shrine. We tengu would never follow orders from a ghost, especially a priest-king ghost."

So. Suzume was at least partly right. "But Lord Chomigoto is the kami of the shrine! My promise to repair it was made to *him*."

"*He* is the kami of that shrine? Oh no!" Goranu doubled over with laughter, holding his stomach.

"Did you not know that?"

"I'm a tengu! We don't pay attention to shrines."

"But you know who Lord Chomigoto is."

"Of course! He wanders our mountain forests and tries to talk to us and order us around. We tengu always just laugh at him."

"So is it not true that a village of his worshipers was destroyed by Lord Tsubushima's clan? Or that Lord Chomigoto's tomb was robbed?"

"Oh yes. All that happened."

"You tengu did nothing to stop the massacre of the village?"

"The horrible things mortals do to one another are none of our affair."

"I see." I paused to consider this a moment. "Then I suppose you would not know or care if Lord Chomigoto would have an association with Lord Emma-O."

"Oh, he almost certainly does. Old Blowhard told us that he begged Emma-O to let him return to this world to seek vengeance or redress or something."

"Oh." My heart sank. "Then he will be able to send Lord Emma-O's demons to fetch me when I fail to do all he has asked."

"He *what?*" Goranu leaped to his feet.

"Lord Chomigoto has demanded that I not only repair his shrine but must make it the greatest the world has ever seen. And that I have the treasures of his tomb restored. And that I gather the descendants of his followers so that he may be venerated once more. He says I must do this because I am descended from the Nakatomi clan, who helped the Yamato overthrow his clan centuries ago."

"That stinking, arrogant, overbearing shade! How dare he! If there is anything a tengu cannot stand it's an arrogant priest, even if he was a king!"

"Then," I said, hope rising once more, "you will help me rebuild the shrine?"

"No. Never. That would only puff him up and make him even more overbearing."

I buried my face in my hands. "Then what am I to do? You were my last hope, Goranu."

He came over and sat down beside me. "So, so. Stop that now. We will not let Old Blowhard do anything to you. But first you must stop thinking like a silly human, being in awe of anyone with noble title or riches. You must start thinking like a tengu. You agree that his demands on you are unjust, don't you?"

"Well, yes."

"Then you must not obey him. But do so in a way that shows Old Blowhard just how foolish he really is. *That* will be justice."

"I do not know how to conceive of such a plan," I said.

"But we tengu excel in such thinking. That is why you must think like us in order to succeed in this."

"But what if Lord Chomigoto realizes he is being tricked and sends Lord Emma-O's demons after me?"

"What if he does?" asked Goranu with a shrug.

"But then I am as lost as I am now, or worse! Why do you not understand this, Goranu?"

Goranu sighed, jumped to his feet, and began to pace the pavilion. "It must be the way you noble girls are raised. Surrounded by walls all the time. So an obstacle rises before you, and all you see is a wall!" He gestured gracefully, and a wood-and-paper wall appeared between us. "To a well-bred noble girl," Goranu continued from the other side, "a wall such as this is impassable. But to creatures like me"—he punched with his fists again and again until the wall was only splintered wood and shredded paper—"there is always a way through." Smiling, he stepped through the hole he had made and bowed to me.

"I should prefer a not so violent solution," I said.

Goranu rolled his eyes. "This was just an example, you silly human! I could have used the ocean and swimming, or a mountain range and flying. My point is that if you respect your obstacle too much, if you give it too much power, here in your mind, you will never overcome it. But if you can see a thing as it really is, learn its nature, then there are always solutions. There is always a way around trouble. Remember that."

It was frightening to realize that there were aspects of the world I could not see because I was not prepared to see them. "But does it matter, if, as we are taught, all the world is illusion?"

Goranu came back and crouched down beside me. "We tengu have learned that for you mortals, much of the illusion is happening up here." He placed his fingertips lightly on my forehead.

"Then how can I see through such illusion?" I asked, wishing, strangely, that he could leave his hand there forever.

Goranu straightened up and looked down at me. "I see I must train you in Tengu-Do, the Way of the Tengu. We tengu are good at teaching warriors, though I must train you in thinking rather than in swordsmanship. You must learn how to fight with your mind. That is the only way you will defeat Old Blowhard and take control of your life again."

Eyes and Ears

A face stares back from

the rain puddle. Who is it?

The eyes are shadowed. . . .

WHEN GORANU and I returned to the tengu village, we found Suzume and Kuroihane seated on a log bench, as far from each other as possible. But they kept stealing sidelong glances at one another. Though I could not be certain, I had the feeling that they had been flirting.

"Suzume-san," Goranu said.

She looked up quickly, startled, as if distracted from a thought. "Hai?"

"Since you are here and we must do something with you, you will come and learn Tengu-Do with your Great Lady Mitsuko."

Kuroihane's eyes widened. "Please, Highness, reconsider. This mortal thinks too much like a tengu already."

97

"Then she may serve as an example to her lady. Come along."

I did not like the idea of Suzume being an example to me in any way, although I had to admit she had been right about some things. "Where are we going?" I asked.

"Another land of illusion, Mitsu-chan, though far different from, and less romantic than, the last." Taking me by one hand and Suzume by the other, Goranu led us to...

I am not permitted to say, exactly, for the tengu like to keep their secrets. But I will describe some things.

There is a grotto, I cannot tell you where, in which the tengu find it easier to do their illusions. It is a large, deep cave, full of glistening rocks and crystal that reflected our torchlight in confusing ways. Even our shadows could not stand still.

Goranu jumped to the top of a large boulder and sat himself upon it, as if he were an incongruous long-nosed, black-robed Buddha. "Now listen well, children, as I reveal to you some of the Way of the Tengu. This must be the short lesson, though, as it usually takes years to teach a mortal what we know.

"There are two rules that Lady Mitsuko must take to heart if she is to overcome her problems. First, take nothing seriously. Second, all things are changeable. Third, there is more and less to everything you see."

Suzume pointed an accusing finger at him. "You said there are two rules, yet you have mentioned three."

"Did I not say all things are changeable? And you should take nothing seriously, not even me. I am just a silly tengu, after all."

I paced back and forth, feeling impatient. "What do these rules have to do with my discharging my debt to Lord Chomigoto?"

Goranu rolled his eyes and shook his head. "You are looking to the way of the warrior, for a sword to cut through your problems. I am offering the way of the magician, to transform your situation so that there is no problem. Just as the swordsman needs to train his arm, the sorcerer must train his mind. Stop pacing like that—you are like a monkey in a cage, and that is more true than you know."

I sat rather ungracefully beside Suzume, in front of Goranu. "What are you talking about? What is true about me and caged monkeys?"

"The world you nobles have created for yourselves—Above the Clouds, as you put it—that is your cage. It is a very pretty cage, to be sure, but it binds you as tightly as ropes. Now I will tell you something that mortals, particularly noble ones, find terrifying. This cage is an illusion. Who you are, what you are, are illusions, and therefore changeable."

I frowned at him. "That is nonsense. I know very well who I am. I am the fourth daughter of my father's branch of the Fujiwara clan."

Goranu shrugged. "An accident of birth. You could have been born a rice cake girl like your servant here, or a farmer, or a bandit. Who would you have been then? What if you had never had nice clothes to wear, never learned to read and write? Wouldn't you be different?"

I blinked. "That makes no sense. I am not those things. I am Fujiwara."

"But should the fortunes of the Fujiwara fall, being a Fujiwara would not mean the same thing at all. You see? All is changeable. It need not be the way it is."

I shook my head. "I do not understand. Not everything is changeable. A person is man or woman, child or adult, noble-born or lowly."

"Oh, some things may be with you from birth: whether you are strong or sickly, shy or bold, quick or slow, cheerful or sullen. But much more is changeable than you know, if one has the will and the way."

Goranu was right; this philosophy was very disturbing if true.

Stubbornly, I said, "From what you say, I should be able to change shape just like you, and I cannot."

Goranu hopped off his rock. "Unlike us tengu, mortals must do their changing in their minds. Sometimes this is reflected in outward appearance, sometimes not. Surely you have seen a Noh play in which actors portray people they are not. Men pretend to be women, and adults pretend to be children."

"I understand!" said Suzume, jumping up. "It is like being a child and pretending things. My brother and I would play at being great warriors or pirates or the Emperor and Empress. Didn't you ever do that, Great Lady?"

I stared at her, shocked. "I would never pretend to be the Empress! Nor would I want to be a pirate or other lowly person."

She, in turn, seemed astonished at me. "You never pretended *anything?*"

"Well, perhaps when I was very, very young. I remember pretending to be a butterfly. But that was childish foolishness."

Goranu shook his head. "Don't you remember when you pretended to be a bosatsu to trick the monks of Mount Hiei into properly burying your brother-in-law?"

"That was your idea, and Dentō's," I grumped. "I would never have thought of such a thing."

"But you were a very willing participant. I would even dare say you enjoyed it. I thought it was very charming of you."

I confess I blushed and hid my face in my sleeves. "I only did it to help Yugiri."

"Hah. You showed great wisdom then. But now you pretend you have forgotten."

Crossing my arms within my sleeves, I complained, "But I cannot play pretend on my own. I am not a child, and I am not an actor."

"All mortals are actors," said Goranu, "whether they know

it or not." He flung his arms wide. "All life is a big Noh play. Hmm. I like that. I must remember that phrase."

"Goranu—"

"Very well, very well. The nub of the matter is this: Sometimes it is useful to be what people expect you to be, but often it can be useful to be someone else—that is, to take on someone else's qualities. Just as I am trying to help you do now. I cannot give you black feathers and wings and a beak. But you might find thinking like a tengu useful. To solve a problem, sometimes you must ignore what you see and what you know and instead choose what will lead to what you want."

I gave him a blank stare. "You are confusing me."

"Argh!" He put his hands to his head in frustration. "Very well. It is time for an example." He did some very complicated gesture, and the three of us were standing on a seashore. I could even smell the salty water and hear the cries of gulls.

Goranu had changed to old-man form, with the shaved head and gray robes of a monk. "Now, you are a fisherman, and I have come from the local temple to beg your catch as a donation. But you need your fish to feed your family. How do you deny me?"

"What?" I said, distracted by the illusion. "But I am not a fisherman."

"I understand! Let me try!" cried Suzume.

"Very well." Goranu turned to her, and his manner changed. He bowed and smiled, his old eyes crinkling. "Good mister fisherman, your family has always been generous to us. Surely, your goodness will bring you great karma. How many baskets full of fish will you be sending to the temple?"

A mischievous expression crossed Suzume's face, and she bowed back to him. "Oh, Good Holy Sir, I am so glad you have come. We have caught very few fish these past days, and I am wondering if our nets are cursed. Won't you say a blessing or two over them while you are here? Surely, I could not insult your temple by sending our poor catch to you."

"Ai, Kuroihane was right. You do already think like us," Goranu muttered under his breath. Then, aloud, he said, "Good fisherman, I am so sorry to hear of your poor catch, and naturally I will bless your nets. But we are very low on food at the temple, and I assure you what few fish you can send us will be greatly appreciated."

Suzume paused, chin in hand, for a moment. Then she said, "Ah!" and bowed again. "Good Holy Sir, I am so glad that we may give these fish to you, for I fear they may be cursed as well. Already two people who have eaten them have fallen sick. But surely the fish will not harm such holy folk as you, and, of course, you have a healer or two at the temple who can handle such matters. Please, take our stinking, unwholesome fish, for who can make better use of them than you?"

"Er, thank you all the same," said Goranu, backing away, "but I would not think to take from you what few fish you have caught. Perhaps some other time."

"Aha!" cried Suzume. "I won!"

"Yes," said Goranu. "But you should not say so while the monk can still hear you. That was excellent, Suzume. You are taking to this very well."

I was annoyed that Suzume seemed to be doing better than I and winning Goranu's approval. "But you are just teaching her to lie!"

"Well, what would you have done?" demanded Suzume.

"I would have given up the fish," I said. "Monks are holy men, and to deny what they ask for brings bad fortune."

"And your family would have starved," said Goranu, "while the monks can always find donations elsewhere. Clearly you are a long way from thinking like a tengu."

"You mean acting any way I please? That is so" — I searched for a word — "undignified."

"Dignity can be useful," said Goranu. "But so can the lack of it. The wisdom is to know when to be what. We have a saying: Chamberlains look very grand in their robes" — Goranu changed into a bureaucrat, wearing the tall black silk hat, voluminous black robes, and trousers whose legs were so long that they trailed behind him — "but they cannot run very fast." Goranu tried to trot across the grotto floor but swiftly tripped and fell.

Suzume giggled behind her hand, and, I confess, I had to laugh as well.

Goranu bounced up and changed back into his long-nosed young-man form. "So you see. Now, another lesson."

And so it went. Goranu would create the illusion of a place and a situation, and Suzume and I would have to solve a problem set there. At first I did poorly, trying to see each problem as I, Fujiwara no Mitsuko, would see it. But with Suzume as an example and with Goranu's urgings, I began to learn just how differently one can see things, how different a person can be, when necessary. It was as though I had been shut in a tower and then a window was opened for me. The view from the window was dizzying, and I did not always like it, but I saw a much wider world.

As we were leaving the grotto, I asked Goranu, "If you tengu are so good at imaginings, why is it you do not paint or write poetry?"

"Because of Rule Number One, Mitsuko. We consider very few things important enough to waste time and feelings for, whereas you mortals shed tears over a sunset or the falling of a cherry blossom."

"What do you consider important, then?" I asked.

Goranu paused and gazed at me. Without speaking, he placed a finger lightly on my cheek. Then he turned and walked ahead to lead us out.

———

By the time we returned to the tengu village, it was already late into the night. The tengu women—homely creatures with clawlike hands, long noses, bedraggled hair, and huge flat feet—were setting bright-colored lanterns outside every hut. I could smell soup and rice cooking, and I felt my stomach growl.

"As you know, we cannot promise you a feast," said Goranu. "But we are willing to feed you, if you don't mind a little stew meat."

"Stew sounds good to me," said Suzume.

I sighed. "It is no wonder you tengu cannot find the Heavenward Path."

"Hey," cautioned Goranu. "No more Buddhist nonsense. I'm through with that. You want to keep your purity, you can chew on grass for dinner. Me, I'm having the stew."

"I wonder what hour it is?" I said to Suzume. "By now I have surely been gone a whole day from Heian Kyō." It seemed so strange. Had it only been that morning that I had spoken to the ghost of Lord Chomigoto? No wonder I felt so very tired.

"Your papa must be really worried by now," said Suzume. "And my family, too."

"Yes. I wish I could see what Papa-san is thinking and doing."

"No, you don't," Goranu chimed in.

"Oh, just a glimpse," I said. "You could show me, couldn't you?"

Goranu crossed his arms on his chest. "I could. But I won't."

"Stubborn tengu," chided Suzume.

"It is for your own good!" said Goranu. "You Buddhists believe you have to give up ties to family, neh? Why is that?"

I stared at the ground and kicked at the dirt. "It is so that one may concentrate on the sacred teachings."

"Exactly. Family problems are distracting. You have much

to contemplate, Mitsuko. You can't be concerned with your papa right now."

I was angry at his dismissive tone, but I said nothing. He was only a tengu, after all. He did not understand important things. Goranu led us into one of the tengu huts, and then he left us. Suzume and I sat on the wooden floor by the plain stone central hearth.

"This is just like my family's old house, only tidier," said Suzume, looking around.

"Is it?" I had spent one night in Suzume's old house, and I shuddered to remember that she was right. Two tengu women came in with bowls of stew that they set down before us. Then they patted our hair and clothes with their clawlike hands.

"How pretty you mortal girls are," one of them cawed at me.

"What lovely hair. And your kimonos, what fine silk they are made of," said the other to Suzume.

"But your noses are so small, poor things."

"And your feet, too. How can you walk with such tiny stubs on the ends of your legs?"

I was getting the feeling that the tengu women would like to tear us to pieces and throw us into the stew pot. "Please leave us," I said. "We would like to eat in peace."

"Ooooh, but of course. We tengu ladies are too lowly for a noblewoman's company."

"Only good enough to be servants, we tengu are. Please forgive our existence." Bobbing and bowing, the tengu women backed out of the hut, glaring at us hatefully.

"Forgive me," said Suzume, "but do you think you could have been a bit more polite? They are feeding us and giving us shelter."

"Why?" I grumbled. "They are hardly polite to each other."

"So? We can be a better example to them."

"They need no examples. They will never change."

"My, we are a stony mountain puddle this evening. The tengu may be sour, but at least they keep their sense of humor. Besides, don't tengu believe everything is changeable?"

"I do not know," I said with a sigh. I lay down on the floor and picked idly at the rough wood grain. "After Goranu's lessons, I hardly know what to think anymore. I will tell you a secret. I used to think that my life would someday be like a monogatari—a beautiful story. But if my problem with Lord Chomigoto had been part of a monogatari, things would be happening very differently."

"A monogatari? You mean those stories you noblewomen write and trade among each other for fun?"

"It is not just amusement. We write about feelings and beauty, the way the world *should* be. If this were one of those stories, the heroine would build the new shrine herself, stone by stone, until her hands bled. And she would walk to the ends of Hokkaido to bring together the last descendants of the villagers. And she would do anything necessary, even sell her family into poverty, to restore the wealth of the ghost-king's tomb."

"Or, more likely, die trying," said Suzume, her mouth full of stew.

"But it would be a noble death," I said, chin on my hands. "A blameless death that led to an honorable heaven, or at least a better rebirth. But instead I lie here in a dilapidated tengu hovel and contemplate baser things."

"Life is never like stories. One thing is clear: No matter how much Goranu trains you, you will still have your head in the Clouds. You and your silly noble ideals."

"Papa once said to lose one's nobility is to allow one's soul to be trampled in the mud. But I see you have adapted to tengu thought very well. You even seemed to trade kind words with Kuroihane, I've noticed."

Suzume sat up straight, her eyes wide. "What! Are you saying I like him? I find him interesting, to be sure, but I am not fond of him. Not like the love you bear your Goranu."

I sat up, too, wishing there were cushions around so I could throw one at her. "I do *not* love Goranu! I feel sorry for him because he studied the sutras for my sake and failed."

"Yes, of course, I must be mistaken," Suzume said dryly, rolling her eyes. "Surely, that is all it is. Only pity. Just as well—for both of us—I suppose. There is no social gain to be had in marrying a tengu."

"Truly, none," I agreed.

"My family would have fits," said Suzume.

"*My* family would disown me. But can you imagine," I said, reclining again on the floor, "what a world would be like where everyone could marry whomever they chose, without thought of social station or what clan they came from? What a strange world that would be—surely, stranger than any world I have visited in my travels."

Suzume shook her head. "That dragon was right about one thing: Given a chance, people will always act foolish and make stupid choices. In my old neighborhood now and then, we would hear about some girl running off with some rogue she had taken a liking to. No good ever came of it that I knew of. My mama says that love is like cherry trees: The blossoms are pretty but they fall off quickly, and you're stuck with stony fruit. It's just as well things are the way they are."

"I am sure you are right," I said, feeling sad.

"Now what I could consider a wonderful world," said Suzume, "is a place where you don't have to spend all day making dinner. Or where your clothes would wash themselves. Or you could have hot water any time you needed it, without having to build a fire and put a kettle on."

"What strange things to wish for," I said.

"That's because you are used to servants doing all that for you. Isn't there anything you don't have that you might like?

Come on, now, imagine this is one of Goranu's problems. Think like a tengu."

"Well, I wish I could create illusions, like the tengu. It would be like writing monogatari, except you could see everything—the clothing, the houses, the beauty of the people. You could choose any kind of story you wanted to see. Or the tengu power of showing you a place far away so you could see what is happening there."

Suzume laughed. "But in a world where anyone might have such powers, you would have to be careful, neh? Somebody might be watching you, without your knowing it."

"Then I would throw a tengu spell so that no one could watch me; only I could watch others."

"But what if everybody had such a spell, so that nobody could watch anybody?"

The argument was becoming so ridiculous, I had to laugh, too. "Then you would have to pass a law that said nobody could use such a spell at certain hours, or that maybe you could only cast voices, but not visions, at certain hours."

"How about smells?" said Suzume. We both fell over with giggles.

"What is the noise in here?" asked Goranu, coming through the curtain door. "A good thing we tengu do not sleep at night, for your chatter would be keeping us all awake."

"We were practicing thinking like tengu," said Suzume.

"And doing very well at it," I added. "We were being very silly and imagining being different sorts of people in a different kind of life."

Goranu raised his brows but said, "I am glad to hear of your progress, for we will start to put your new thinking to use tomorrow. Therefore, I suggest you both get some sleep. I don't want to be dealing with fuzzy heads in the morning."

"Goranu," I said, "what if...what if Lord Chomigoto

should speak to me in my dreams again? I may not be able to sleep if I fear that will happen."

"If he does," said Goranu, "then you must talk back to him in your dream. You must tell him that you are staying with us and that you are working on your tasks. That should satisfy him. And," Goranu added with a wink, "it will make him worry." He turned to go when Kuroihane entered through the curtain, carrying two rolled-up mats of thick, soft reeds.

"I brought these," said Kuroihane, bowing, "because you ladies are used to finer things than sleeping on a hard floor."

"You are going to spoil them," Goranu said.

"Oh no, Highness," said Kuroihane. "This way they will not ruin the nice wood floors with their lint and hair. Mustn't have the place smelling of humans after they are gone. And we can burn the mats later."

"How very thoughtful of you," Suzume said with narrowed eyes. "This way your wood floors will not leave splinters in our hair and skin."

"Or tear our delicate silk kimonos," I added.

"Do you dare to insult our fine dwellings?" said Kuroihane.

"I think I shall leave," said Goranu mildly, "before war is declared. Good night."

"As will I," said Kuroihane, dropping the mat rolls. "Clearly, the ladies need their sleep, as they are getting snappish. Good night."

Both tengu bowed and departed. Suzume and I rolled out the mats on the floor.

"I think," said Suzume, "that despite all our practice, I will never manage to think as tengu do."

"Perhaps it is just as well," I said. I lay down on my mat as Suzume extinguished the lamps. I did not believe that I would fall asleep quickly, but I must have been very tired, because I did. Lord Chomigoto did not speak in my dreams, but the mysterious woman in the old-fashioned, bulky kimonos did. Somehow I knew she was singing, even though I could not see her face or hear her words. She had a sakaki branch in each hand and waved them as she danced through the forest. It was a very soothing dream.

I awoke to see long daggers of sunlight on the floor, slipping in under the curtain door. Sitting up, I rubbed my eyes and yawned, trying to remember where I was and why.

Suzume pushed aside the curtain and stepped into the hut, holding a wooden tray. "Ah, good, you are awake. Say what you will about those tengu women, they're pretty good cooks. I brought us some breakfast."

"Good morning to you, too," I murmured. I took the covered bowl Suzume handed me and lifted off the lid. I saw rice in a bean broth topped with...chopped egg. "If the tengu are bird people," I said, "how is it they can eat egg?"

"I asked them," said Suzume, "and they told me some humans eat monkey meat, so we are not fit to judge."

"I would never eat monkey meat," I said, picking up a pair of chopsticks from the tray.

Suzume shrugged and held her bowl up to her mouth and began to shovel the rice in with her chopsticks.

Clearly, she has not yet learned that a lady, even a lady's maid, does not eat too much or too eagerly, I thought. But I was hungry, too, and so I ate mine, though a little more slowly, egg and all.

I had almost finished when Goranu walked in, followed by Kuroihane. They bowed, and Goranu said, "Good morning, ladies. Did you sleep well?"

"Like a stone," said Suzume.

"What, lumpy and cold with ants crawling beneath you?" asked Kuroihane.

"No, blind, deaf, and impervious to the antics of silly creatures like you," she replied.

"I slept very well," I said, careful not to say anything Goranu could make a joke on.

"Good," said Goranu. "No spirits haunted your dreams, then?"

"Not Lord Chomigoto. There was a woman in old-fashioned clothing whom I did not recognize. She sang and danced, waving sakaki branches, but I don't know why I dreamed of her."

"Hmmm," said Goranu, rubbing his chin. "We tengu normally don't interpret mortal dreams. They are too strange for us. But I would guess that this woman might be some sort of ancestral spirit protecting you."

Somehow Goranu's guess did not feel right, but I did not choose to contradict him.

"But what do I know?" Goranu went on. "I'm just a silly tengu, after all. Now to this morning's tasks. You, Kuroihane, will take Suzume-san and teach her those things I discussed with you last night."

"Must I suffer more of her company, Highness?"

"You must. It is your just punishment for being rude to Great Lady Mitsuko yesterday."

"But I'm a tengu. I'm supposed to be rude to pompous nobility. And she was behaving pompously, Highness."

"That doesn't matter," said Goranu. "In the future, be more careful about whom you choose to annoy. Now go."

"You did not ask me," said Suzume, "as to whether I would agree to be taught by Kuroihane."

"No," said Goranu, smiling. "I did not."

For a moment, they stared at one another, and then Suzume said, "Hmpf!" and left the hut with Kuroihane.

"Are you finished with your meal?" Goranu asked me. "Good. Will you come walk with me?"

"Of course," I said. We left the hut and strolled down the main path of the village. All was quiet and peaceful. The air smelled of cool, wet grasses and pine, and birds chirped pleasantly in the distance.

"Now that you have practiced thinking like a tengu," said Goranu, "have you applied it to your own problem? Have you considered what you must do next?"

"I have tried to think on it," I said, "but it is like ice on a warm day, slippery and hard to grasp."

"Sometimes there are reasons why a thought eludes one. Sometimes it is fear. What is it that you fear most? What is the worst that Lord Chomigoto could do to you?"

"He could deliver me to the demons of Lord Emma-O."

"Very well. Now you must step back from the fear, for to think like a tengu, you must take nothing seriously. What is Lord Emma-O?"

"He...he is a Great Kami. A god."

"That is taking him too seriously. Try again."

"He is Judge of the Dead."

"He is what?"

I sighed, losing patience. "I said he is Judge—"

"That's enough! Think about what you just said."

"That he is a judge?"

"If someone in your city is likely to bring an unjust suit against you, what do you do?"

"I...I am not sure. If it is an ordinary judge, my family would doubtless speak to him on my behalf to explain my side."

"Alas, your family cannot speak for you this time. But wouldn't you say Lord Chomigoto's claim against you is unjust?"

"Of course!"

"Do you not deserve to be heard, then, by the judge who would hear his claim?"

I stopped. "You are saying I must go speak to Lord Emma-O myself. Before Lord Chomigoto does."

Goranu turned and looked at me. "You are showing promise."

I began to protest. "But—"

Goranu raised his brows.

I sighed again. "You are right. If I tried to appease Lord Chomigoto, he might only demand more of me or my family. Nothing will be solved unless I can deflect the sword he points at me."

Goranu smiled. "There is the brave Mitsuko I know."

I looked down at the ragged hems of my kimonos. "No, I am not brave. I must tell you that I am very frightened by all of this, even if I know it is what I must do."

"That shows you are not a complete fool. Do you know how warriors deal with their fear?"

"How could I? I have never been a warrior."

"They banish their fear of death by accepting it. They assume that death will be their fate, and they resolve to die in the best way possible. If they should happen to live through their battle"—Goranu shrugged—"they resolve to continue doing their best, for death will surely come sometime."

"I see," I said, not feeling reassured.

"Mind you," Goranu continued, "a tengu would never be so cold-blooded. When we fight, we know we will win. If we don't think we're going to win, we run away. That's because we're more sensible than mortals."

"But I don't know that I will win."

"Is your cause not just?"

"Well, yes, but—"

"Is Lord Emma-O not just?"

"It is said he is, but—"

"Then how can you fail?"

I realized I had no answer to that. "Very well. You are right. Let us go to your Esteemed Ancestor, Susano-wo, so that he may again deliver me to the court of Lord Emma-O."

Goranu began to laugh, holding his sides.

"What is so funny?"

Between laughing and gasping, he said, "You are. I am. I should be angry at you for your arrogance, and yet...and yet...it is so like a tengu."

I did not know what to say. "Forgive me then if it seems arrogant, but it is the only way, neh?"

Goranu fell on his rear end onto the ground, still chuckling. "I am sorry, Most Noble and Beauteous Mitsuko, but what you ask is not possible. My Esteemed Ancestor is not beneath the island of Eno right now."

"Why...oh. Now I remember. All the kami, it is said, go to Izumo this month for their conference."

"Smart girl. Now you understand."

"But, then it is simple. You must fly me to Izumo, and I will speak to Susano-wo there instead."

Goranu again roared with laughter until I felt quite at a loss. "*Now* what is funny?"

"Hoo, hoo, hoo, think about it! All the Great Kami in one place! Hoo! Hoo! Hoo!"

"You mean...oh, I see! If all the kami are there, then Lord Emma-O will be, too, and I won't need the help of your Esteemed Ancestor!"

Goranu nodded and pointed at me, his face red as bean paste from laughing.

"But still I must get to Izumo, somehow. So you must fly me there. Is it not right that I get there as soon as possible to plead my case?"

With deep gasps, Goranu labored to control his laughing. "Think of it. All the Great Kami. Izunami and Izunagi. Amaterasu herself. All there. And a little mortal girl. Comes flying in. On the back of a tengu. And says, 'I would like to speak to Lord Emma-O, if you please.'" Laughter overtook him once more, and Goranu curled up on his side on the ground.

I watched him some moments, trying to fight back my anger. "This is just like the last time, isn't it? When I wanted to pound on the gates of Hiei-zan and demand that the warrior priests properly bury Yugiri. You showed me then that I would only be making a fool of myself and that I would fail."

Goranu sat up. "Ah. You *are* learning."

"But I still do not understand! You will not be harmed by flying into Izumo. If you, a prince of the tengu, introduced me to the kami, surely they would listen."

Goranu sighed and shook his head, resting his cheek in his hand. "It warms my heart that you think so highly of me. But again, you must reduce the scene to understand it. If you were to request audience with a high official at the Imperial Court in Heian Kyō, would you ride up to the gate on a large dog? You would be laughed away, would you not? For that is how the Great Kami view us lesser demons, as you view dogs or worse. No." Goranu stood and dusted himself off. "You are a Great Lady, and you ought to be received as such."

"I see. It is as the head nun, Tadashi, said at the temple. A lady is known by what she surrounds herself with."

"Surprising wisdom, for a nun."

"Stop that. Very well. I should travel to Izumo by something more...impressive. But a fine carriage would be too slow, even if I could get one. Could we do an illusion of an imperial ox-carriage?"

"Don't you think the Great Kami could see right through a tengu illusion?"

"Oh. Yes. I suppose they could."

"I would suggest something far more likely to gain their attention." Goranu turned his head and gazed toward the cloud-shrouded mountain that overlooked the village.

"You . . . you mean the dragon Kai-Lung? Do you think he would do that?"

"I don't know. You will have to ask him."

I fiddled with my sleeves anxiously. "Well, but he is angry at me. But, then, if *you* ask, surely he will listen to you—"

"Haven't you heard anything I've been saying?" Goranu shouted at me. "Awk! Sometimes I think I have taught you nothing!" Feathers began to sprout from his head and hands. "So. Very well. This shall be the test of whether you have mastered Tengu-Do. You alone must go up the mountain. And you will speak to Kai-Lung. And you will convince him to fly you to Izumo. If you return, having failed to do this, none of us will speak to you again, for you will be unworthy of the company of tengu. This is your task, Mitsuko-san. Go."

I stepped back, stunned. "Goranu?"

He turned his back to me. "Speak no more. Go!"

Astonished, angry, and hurt all at once, I lifted the hems of my kimonos and trudged toward the mountain path.

Contact

Lovely butterfly
flits to and fro, but always
just out of my reach.

I STOMPED UP the mountainside, hardly able to see the path for the tears blurring my sight. Why was everyone being so unfair to me? First my father, demanding that I marry a child-prince. Then Lord Chomigoto. And now Goranu, whom I trusted more than anyone else in the world.

Perhaps, said a small voice inside me, Goranu has sent you to do this because he trusts that you will not fail. He has said he loves you, after all. Or perhaps, said a different voice within, he was so discouraged by my poor abilities in Tengu-Do, that he no longer cares, and if I fail to get Kai-Lung's help—or worse, I am killed by the dragon—Goranu will be rid of my troubling presence.

Alas, the thought that Goranu might no longer care was more painful than all the rest. Indeed, so sad was the thought that it stopped my tears. A change blew over me like an icy wind, and I felt myself become cold inside. My feet moved of themselves, and I put no thought to my steps, as if I were merely a rider inside my body. I took little notice of the mist closing in around me, or the wet grasses slapping at my ankles. I no longer cared what Kai-Lung might do to me.

> Is this what it means
> to have a warrior's heart
> that cannot fear death?

But even numb as I was, there came a point when I could walk no further, and I sank down onto a low stone.

It was an extraordinary experience, to feel so empty of cares. There was freedom in it. The gray mist around me seemed friendly. I welcomed its dampness and chill.

I do not know how long I sat there, contemplating not-feeling, when I saw flickering orange lights within the mist, and the kirin emerged on the path in front of me.

"Oh!" it said in its piping voice. "It is you. Hello again."

I bowed where I sat. "Good day to you. I have returned to speak once more with Kai-Lung."

"Oh, dear, dear," said the kirin, dipping its horned head in a bow. "Forgive me, but I must tell you that is impossible. After the disturbance yesterday, Kai-Lung declared that he wished to see no more mortals for a very long time. I would advise you not to wait."

I stared at the kirin, surprised at the dismay-that-I-did-not-feel. A strange mood swept over me then, as if another spirit had suddenly lodged within me. I stepped forward and then flung myself to the ground in front of the kirin. "But that is the very reason I am here!" I wailed, nearly convincing myself of my despair. "I have come to offer apologies for my abominable behavior yesterday. I have not slept this past night, I was so filled with guilt and sorrow. You must let me abase myself to

Kai-Lung. I will offer him anything; I will be his servant—offer my whole family as servants—to pay for the insult I have done him. If I cannot see him, I do not think I can live with my shame."

I sat up and took a twig from the ground. I held it against my neck as if it were a knife. "If I cannot see Kai-Lung, my only recourse will be to take my own life in dishonor."

"Oh, dear, dear, dear," muttered the kirin, dancing nervously on its little hooves. "Please do not do that, you mustn't. That would be a terrible thing. I am sure Kai-Lung will be reasonable and understanding when I tell him what you have come for. Please wait right here. Don't move. I will be right back. Oh, dear, dear, dear..." The kirin turned around and delicately trotted up the mountain into the mist.

When it had gone, I felt...giddy. I wanted to bubble into laughter, even though I felt no happiness inside. *Is this part of tengu nature?* I wondered. But I sat still and let no emotion show in case someone might be watching.

Presently, the kirin returned, nearly bouncing on its tiny hooves. "I bring good news! Kai-Lung has agreed to speak with you, seeing that it's only you and not your spiteful servant. Come along, then! Make haste! Who knows how long he will be in this forbearing mood? Come, come. Hurry along."

I followed the kirin up the hillside, stepping carefully over the stones-that-might-be-scales, until again I stood in the fog-shrouded clearing where I had spoken to Kai-Lung before. Again I waited, not caring how long I had to stand.

But soon the mighty head of the dragon emerged from the fog in front of me. "I am told," rumbled Kai-Lung, "that you have come to beg forgiveness of me."

"I have, Most Wise One," I said, bowing deeply. "What you told me yesterday is true. I have been a great fool."

Kai-Lung's eyes widened. "Well! You have had a change of heart indeed. Rare are the mortals who will admit to their failings so readily. I will give you the chance to make amends. What do you offer me in exchange for my forgiveness?"

I stared into the dragon's enormous golden eye, the pupil dark and deep as a well. I felt as though Kai-Lung could see into me perhaps as clearly. Lies or trickery in the tengu manner would be fruitless, or even dangerous, and, worst of all, insulting. This was a time when only the truth would do. "I wish to offer you, Great Kai-Lung, a story."

The dragon raised his head suddenly, but in surprise, not anger. "A story? That is unusual. Not gold or silk or lifetime service?"

"Gold and silk may be stolen from you, and the life of a mortal is short compared to yours. But a story can remain in your memory to give you pleasure forever, Great Kai-Lung."

"Assuming it is a good story," said the dragon. "Good stories are a treasure, indeed."

"I am pleased that you think so, for it is all I have to give. I will begin, if you will permit me."

There came a rumbling around me as if the whole mountain were shifting, changing position. Two enormous talons appeared beneath the dragon's head, and Kai-Lung crossed them, then laid his long chin down on them. He slowly blinked and sighed and said, "Begin."

And so I told him the same tale that I have written here— about Lord Chomigoto and my promise to repair the shrine. Even about Goranu, for I felt it unwise to omit anything. Even about my being sent back to Kai-Lung to request a ride to Izumo. It had become late afternoon by the time I stopped speaking and bowed.

"Hmmm?" said Kai-Lung. "But this story has not ended!"

"No," I agreed, "it has not. And my further gift to you is that you may decide, Great Kai-Lung, how it ends."

"Mmmm. You are a clever girl. This is an irresistible gift, as you must surely know. Were you to disappear from my sight this moment, I would still be wondering how it would end, perhaps forever. Mmmm. In some sorts of stories, it might end with my killing or eating you."

"That is so," I agreed.

"But such stories stem from unkind humor and offer no wisdom or enlightenment. I will not choose such an end."

I confess, I did feel some relief when he said this.

"Then again," Kai-Lung went on, "in some stories, I would simply send you away, and you would have to wander back to Heian Kyō, perhaps to be kidnapped by brigands or disowned by an angry father. You might hide yourself away in some old, rotting house, as is so fashionable in the monogatari these days, until you faded away into some skeletal spirit to keep company with the mice and frighten those who happen upon you."

"I have seen such stories, too, Great One."

"Hm. Well, I don't like them. Too melancholy, too wallowing in sorrowful feelings. And again, there is no moral, no uplifting message. A useless sort of story. No, I will not choose that sort of end, either."

I was pleased to hear this, as well. "What sort of end would the Great Kai-Lung like to see?"

"There is only one direction the story may go that is right and proper. You have suffered injustice, therefore justice must be served. You must, indeed, speak to Lord Emma-O in Izumo. And since your tengu friend is being typically cowardly and selfish, you will have to get there some other way."

"Yes?"

"And since I, myself, dearly wish to know how this story will end—and the only way I can be sure to know that is if I witness it myself—then I am naturally the one to take you there."

"That does seem reasonable," I said, filling with hope.

"Then I have decided," said Kai-Lung. "I will take you to Izumo. But not as you are. You are a bedraggled, sorry, wretched sight, and I will not have such a creature on my back in front of all the Great Kami. Come into my cave, and we will see if we can make you more presentable."

Kai-Lung's head withdrew into the mist, and a light appeared in front of me. I followed the light, and it led me into a huge, open cavern. I gasped in astonishment, for the light revealed a cave filled with jewels, gold and silver, swords and lances and armor, embroidered kimonos, mirrors of bronze, treasures everywhere I looked.

"People keep giving me these things," grumbled Kai-Lung. "I do not know what they think I will do with them. I have no need for gold or weapons or clothing. I am glad you offered me an intangible—a story—as it won't add to the clutter. Just this morning, some monks left me some rice and pickled vegetables as an offering. As if that is what dragons eat! You can have it, if you like. It's over there by the jade mask."

"Thank you," I said, for I suddenly realized I was very hungry. I went to the mask the dragon indicated and found the covered bowl. The rice and pickles were still wholesome, so I sat down on a fine lacquered chest and ate a bit. It was very strange to be sitting amid wealth that surely equaled the Emperor's, and yet I was not impressed by it. Instead, it struck me as seeming rather silly, as if too much effort had been put into things that were unimportant. Of course, that is what they had been trying to teach me all along at Sukaku Temple.

After I had finished eating, Kai-Lung showed me where there were combs and mirrors and long golden hairpins so that I could make myself presentable. He even gave me fine kimonos of white silk and a grand outer kimono embroidered with gold and silver threads in a pattern of clouds and cranes.

"That is much better," said Kai-Lung when I had finished dressing. "You are no longer an embarrassment."

From what glimpses I could get of myself in the polished bronze mirror, I was quite amazed. No one outside of the Imperial Family would wear such finery as I had on. It was fortunate I was not going to Court, or there would be much wagging of tongues, I am sure.

"Darkness has fallen," said Kai-Lung. "Now is a good time to leave. If you are ready."

"I am ready," I said, although I was not sure if this was true. I walked out of the cave and peered around me. It was no longer quite so misty, but the dim twilight made it hard to see. I wondered just how I would get onto the dragon's back and how I would ride.

"Climb up those rocks over there," said Kai-Lung. "And then you will see my back ridge spines."

Very carefully, so as not to damage the gold-embroidered outer kimono I wore, I climbed the stones. At the top, I saw flat scales ahead of me and a row of tall, slanting poles which must have been the spines he mentioned. I walked awkwardly across his scales and sat myself between two of the spines—there was plenty of room—and held on to the one in front of me.

"Are you settled?" Kai-Lung's enormous head rose up some ways ahead of me and turned to look back at me.

"Yes, I am prepared!" I called back to him.

"Hang on, then."

It seemed the whole mountain began to move beneath and around me. Wind blew at my face, and suddenly we were in the air. I looked down, hoping to see the tengu village, but there were only dim clouds below. I wished at least Goranu could see me. I wanted to shout down to him, "Look, Goranu! I have done it! Kai-Lung is flying me to Izumo. I was worthy of your teaching after all." But if he no longer cared, perhaps he was not even watching.

Once Kai-Lung was high off the mountain, it was almost as though we were not in motion at all. Had there not been cold air rushing against my face, I would have thought that the dim land below was scrolling by me and that I was sitting still. It was a quite different experience from when I flew on Goranu's back. Instead of warm, soft feathers, I sat on cold, hard scales. I felt much safer, but it was not nearly so exciting. Kai-Lung's body was so wide that I could not see much of the ground. The sky had gotten so dark that there was little to see—only a glow of purple in the sky behind the western mountains. The stars, however, were magnificent. I leaned back against the spine behind me and stared up at them for a long time.

I wonder if I can see the Lover's Bridge, I thought, *and the two stars that are the separated lovers. How sad that, if the tale is true, they can only meet once a year. How fortunate,* thought another part of me, *that they can meet at all.*

We flew west and a little north. I had heard that Izumo was far away to the west of Heian Kyō, so we must have been flying fast, but I could not tell. My hands and face felt quite cold, but I did not care.

At last, Kai-Lung called back, "We are there. Look down and see." He turned his body so that I sat at an angle, but I could see nothing but darkness below, and I said so.

"Ah. Of course. I forgot. One moment." Kai-Lung snapped his mighty tail far behind me, and thunder pealed across the sky. His body shuddered, and suddenly, below, I saw an enormous shrine with a high, steep roof and a tall torii gate. The shrine glowed with a golden light, as if built from the sun itself. "There it is," said Kai-Lung. "The meeting place of the Great Kami."

We circled it, flying lower and lower, and I was amazed at the shrine's size and beauty. I felt insignificant indeed, and I was not sure even Kai-Lung would help me to be noticed here. Goranu was right, as he had so often been. I wished I could apologize to him.

Kai-Lung landed some distance from the shrine. I hardly knew when we had touched the ground. He walked up to the huge broad courtyard in front of the shrine and crouched close to the ground. Even so, I was still high up, and I feared harming myself if I jumped or slid down. "How do I get off of you?"

"I will help." Kai-Lung lifted his enormous foot up close to me, and I scrambled onto it. He lowered the talon onto the ground slowly, and I was able to simply step off.

The courtyard was lit with round lanterns set up on high poles. I wondered how they were illuminated, as no candles or wicks I had ever seen burned so bright.

"It must be that Amaterasu is here," said Kai-Lung. "She Who Is the Sun lends her brilliance everywhere."

"Ah, I understand," I said. I hoped I would not encounter her, for surely I would be blinded. "Thank you," I called up to the dragon. His head towered over me.

"Let us now see if we can finish your story," he rumbled. "Here come our greeters."

Three guardian oni approached, and ugly demons they were, too. They each had three eyes and two horns on their foreheads. Their skins were gray. They each carried a mallet in one hand and a spiked iron rod in the other. They wore only tiger-pelt loincloths. Bobbing their heads, they approached us with caution.

"You would be welcome, Mighty Kai-Lung," said the lead oni, "but this is a mortal, and she cannot come here."

"You fool!" roared Kai-Lung. "Do you not see that this is Great Lady Fujiwara no Mitsuko of the clan who are Guardians of the Sacred Mirror? She does not desire to mingle with the kami. But a great injustice has been done her, and she must speak with Lord Emma-O at once!"

The oni stepped back, watching me warily. "No mortal may disturb the conference of the kami."

"Then let it be known," rumbled Kai-Lung, "that I request that Lord Emma-O come forth on her behalf. And that if he does not, I will rend the air above the shrine with thunder so loud and so long that no kami will be able to hear another. Tell them so!"

All three oni jumped back. "As you wish," the lead one said. He turned to me. "But it will go hard on you if Lord Emma-O is displeased."

I simply stared at him, saying nothing and making no gesture. After a few moments, he and the other oni turned and scurried off through the great gateway to the shrine.

"What if Lord Emma-O is displeased with you?" I asked Kai-Lung. "Are you not afraid?"

"Hah. Dragons are outside his jurisdiction, you might say. If he has a problem with any of us, he must speak to Ryujin-sama. And King Ryujin never listens to the other kami."

"Is Ryujin-sama here, also, then?"

"I could not tell you. He follows his own whims. Ah, that was swift."

The great gateway swung open again, and two horse-headed oni came out. Right behind them was a tall man with a coarse beard. He wore a black robe and bureaucrat's hat and carried a long staff with two faces carved on it. It was difficult to watch him, for he would appear, disappear, and reappear again, like the light of a firefly. Goranu had once explained to me that naturally the Great Judge must flicker like this, for he had many courts in which to simultaneously preside, and the work of the Lord of Death never ceases.

"I had thought such pranks beneath your kind, Kai-Lung," intoned the Lord of Death.

"It is no prank, O-sama. Behold your petitioner."

The Lord of Death's gaze fell on me, and suddenly his eyes glowed red. "YOU!" To the oni, he said, "Arrest her!"

Suddenly, one of Kai-Lung's enormous claws encircled me. "Stay back!" he roared at the oni. "Or I will claim her soul in the name of Ryujin-sama, as is the right of the Clan of Dragons with any who are of noble blood in this land."

"You would interfere with justice?" asked Lord Emma-O.

"It is in the name of justice that we are here, O-sama. You are being misused. Your reputation as a righteous judge is in peril. Do you not wish to hear how this may have come about?"

"Very well," said Lord Emma-O. Again he stared at me. "Speak."

It took me a moment to find my voice. I felt very, very small beneath the Lord of Death's gaze, and it took all my courage to force any sound out of my throat. "You know of one, O Great Lord, who is called Lord Chomigoto?" I squeaked.

Lord Emma-O turned to one of the oni, who pulled out of the air an enormous scroll. After unrolling it at an impossible speed, the Lord of Death said at last, "Yes. What of him?"

I explained, in a halting voice, what Lord Chomigoto had asked of me and why, and how he threatened me with Lord Emma-O's wrath if I did not comply.

The Lord of Death held up his hand and said, "It is entirely inappropriate that I hear anything more about this case now. This is not a court, and the accused is not present to answer to the charges. If you wish me to address this matter, you will have to appear before me in my judgment chamber. Since you have been there before," he said with a stern nod, "I assume you can find it again."

"But if I show up in your judgment chamber," I protested, "I would be trespassing again!"

"Indeed," said Kai-Lung. "And what is to keep you from arresting her the moment she returns to your chamber?"

"If her case is sufficiently interesting," said Lord Emma-O, "I will hear it first, before taking other action. If it is justice she truly seeks, she will not be afraid to face me in the proper place. That is all I will say on this matter." Without another word, the Lord of Death turned on his heel and strode back to the shrine gate. The oni sneered at me and then went trotting after him. One of the demons stopped and sniffed at something beyond the light cast by the lanterns. I looked but saw nothing except blackness. The oni saw nothing as well, apparently, and continued on through the gate.

"Hmpf. How frustrating," grumbled Kai-Lung.

"Yes." I sighed. "Now I do not know what to do."

"Now I will not see the end of the story," the dragon said. "Unless..."

"Yes?" I turned and looked up at him.

"What I told O-sama was true, and I can still make that offer. If you wish, Mitsuko-san, I can take you to King Ryujin's Kingdom Under the Sea. There you may live out the rest of your days in a place of great beauty and peace. And even after your body has passed on, your soul may remain, for Ryujin-sama looks after his noble guests."

"But I can never return to this world if I go to the Kingdom Under the Sea."

"No, or if you did, you might find decades or centuries had passed."

I nodded. "I thank you for your kind offer, Great Kai-Lung, but I am not ready to leave all that I have known here, or to give up my place on the next turn of the Wheel."

"I understand. Although the offer was more selfish than you think, since if you did accept, I would then be satisfied in knowing the end to your story. But what will you do now?"

"I do not think I can go back to the tengu village. Goranu will not be impressed that I failed to charm Lord Emma-O. If I were to go home, I do not know how furious my father would be, and I might still have to marry the boy-prince. And nothing would be solved, and Lord Chomigoto might still curse my family and convince O-sama that I am guilty of breaking my promise. I suppose," I said at last, feeling a heavy weight inside, "that I must do as Lord Emma-O demands and meet him again in his judgment chamber, no matter what happens afterward."

"Hmmm," said Kai-Lung. "You are a most extraordinary

mortal, that is clear. I will do this much more for you: I will fly you to the entrance to his realm. That much is in my power, and I can stay with your story that much longer. From there, however, you are on your own."

"I thank you for all your help. Yes, we had best go right away, before I become too afraid."

He lifted me up on his palm, and again I seated myself on his broad, scaly back.

> *A cold autumn wind*
> *blows the moth into the fire*
> *that she sought for warmth.*

Sensation

Finding a seashell,
I lose myself in its coils
spiraling inward....

I DO NOT KNOW in what direction we flew. Gradually, the sky became lighter and lighter—but it was not the light of day. The whole sky became gray, but not the gray of clouds. Just...gray. The landscape below us was barren, treeless hills and jagged canyons.

In time, we came to a river of roiling gray water. Three roads led up to the river, each road choked with people whose skin and clothing were gray. They must be the souls of the dead, I realized.

The three roads crossed the river in different places, and each crossing was different from the other. The left-most road ended at the riverbank, and the waters beyond rose in huge waves in which monsters lurked. The unhappy souls who crossed there shrieked in fear, and I noticed that not all of them reached the other side. The middle road led to a gentle ford in the river, with stepping-stones across. Those souls who crossed there only had the difficulty of jumping from stone to stone—sometimes slipping and falling but getting no more than a little wet. The right-most road had a golden bridge spanning the river, on which happy souls crossed with ease.

"I will set you down by the bridge," said Kai-Lung, "near the saintly ones. You will be safer there, and I believe from there you will find an easier passage into Lord Emma-O's court."

"Thank you," I said. "That is very kind of you."

The gray souls hardly seemed to notice us as we landed on the broad, sandy bank of the river, just beyond the golden bridge. I rode down to the ground on Kai-Lung's paw, and he said, "You must promise me...No, too many promises have been demanded of you already. If you have the opportunity, I would appreciate hearing how your story ends."

I bowed low to him. "It is the least I can offer you in return for your help. If I have the chance, I will gladly tell you all."

"Good luck to you, Fujiwara no Mitsuko." Kai-Lung leaped into the air and, with a snap of his tail, disappeared in a mighty clap of thunder.

I stood beside the river for some moments, listening to the rush of its waters and the soft murmuring of the souls nearby. A ways ahead of me there stood a cliff with an enormous cavern entrance. I watched the souls going in and tried to gather my courage to join them. In time, I became aware of a crowd of gray-faced, gray-garmented people gathering around me. Some wore the flowing robes of the nobility, some the plain robes of monks and nuns, while many wore the simple jackets and leggings of farmers and fishermen. The souls of the dead stared at me with wide eyes, and pressed closer and closer.

"She is alive!" whispered one of them.

"She does not belong here," said another.

"P-please pardon me," I began, as an old-woman spirit reached out to touch my sleeve.

"Do not be afraid," said the old woman. "We will not harm you. But you should not be here. This is not a place for the living. You should leave at once."

"I cannot," I said. "I have business with Lord Emma-O, who invited me himself to his chamber of judgment."

A gasp traveled among the spirits of the dead. "By yourself? A young girl? A living soul in the Court of the Dead? What terrible fate has brought you to this?"

"An ancient wizard-king spirit claims that I owe him a great debt, but I feel what he asks is unfair. Lord Emma-O must decide if what the spirit demands is just."

"Oh, poor dear," said the old-woman spirit. "I have heard that Lord Emma-O, while just, is very strict. He is not known to be merciful."

"Nonetheless," I said, "it is what I must do."

"Surely, there is some way we can help her," said an old-man spirit nearby.

"Yes, yes," whispered the spirits among themselves. "We must help her."

I wondered that these departed souls would feel so moved to help one who was not even related to them. But then I remembered Kai-Lung had set me down among the saintly ones. "You are all kind to think so, but you do not know whether I am worthy of your assistance. I cannot ask you to delay your progress for my sake."

The old woman chuckled. "If we paused to determine whether someone we help is worthy, we might argue forever."

"Besides," said the old man, "even an unworthy one might have a change of heart someday and become worthy. One can never know."

"Now what shall we do?" asked another spirit. "Are you, by any chance, a Buddhist?"

"Yes, I am," I replied. "Of the Tendai sect."

"That is very good," said another. "In that case, we can call a bosatsu to help you."

"Yes!" said the old woman. "We must summon Jizo to take her side."

"Indeed!" said the old man. "Jizo is the very one to help her."

"I beg your pardon," I said, "but although I remember Jizo's name from my studies at the temple, I do not recall why he would be particularly helpful to me."

"Why, Jizo loves arguing with Lord Emma-O on any soul's behalf. He will be the perfect advocate for you." At that, all the gray people around me bowed their heads and began to chant, "Jizo, Jizo, Jizo..." in the manner of monks, for some of them had been monks and nuns while they lived. I felt deeply honored that they would do this for me and sad that I could never return their kindness.

Part of the sky directly above us turned to golden light, and a figure appeared in it. He wore a red cloak and held in one hand the thin staff mendicant priests carry, and in the other hand he held a polished jewel. His head was shaved in the manner of monks. He stepped down through the air as if it had been carved into steps, until he was standing on the riverbank among us.

"Who is it who calls to me?" the bosatsu said in a sweet-toned, very pleasant voice.

The saintly spirits all bowed very low, and I did the same. "We have called you, most blessed Jizo, on behalf of this living spirit who has found her way here. She is in most extraordinary circumstances and needs your guidance."

"Does she?" Jizo said, turning his benign gaze on me. "What has happened to you, young Lady?"

I told him briefly of my promise at the Shinto shrine,

and Lord Chomigoto's demands and his threat to use Lord Emma-O's demons against me.

"Ah," Jizo said. "It is good that you have called for me, for Lord Emma-O is often more mindful of contracts than personages. Such an entanglement as yours will interfere with your finding the Path, and I have no wish to see a pious soul suffer so. I will go with you into O-sama's court. Come, follow me."

As he turned, I bowed to the saintly ones. "Thank you again. You have been most helpful."

They bowed in return. "You are most welcome," they murmured. "May good fortune follow you."

I hurried after Jizo, who in his bright red cloak was easy to see amid the gray people. He led me up the huge cavern opening, when suddenly a deranged-looking old hag stepped out right in front of me.

"I am Kawa no Toshionna! Give me your clothes!"

I jumped back, startled. "What? Why?"

"No one passes into the Realm of the Dead with their worldly goods on their back! Give me your clothes, or I shall tear them off you!" She held up hands like claws.

Jizo walked up behind her and said softly in her ear, "Look again, old woman. This one isn't dead."

"Impossible! Ridiculous!"

"No, it is true," I said. "I am quite alive."

"Then you shouldn't be here!"

"But I must. I must speak to Lord Emma-O in his chamber."

"Well. You can't go in with your clothes on. Give me your clothes! Unless...you happen to have some coins on you."

I looked at Jizo helplessly, but he only sighed and rolled his eyes. I said to the old woman, "I have no money. But this outer kimono is sewn with gold and silver threads. Will you take that?" Somewhat embarrassed because of the other souls nearby, I removed the outermost kimono that Kai-Lung had given me and handed it to the old woman.

She sniffed at it, poked at it, then stuffed it under one arm. "It'll do. Go on." She walked around me, and I heard her accost some other poor soul behind me. "I am Kawa no Toshionna! Give me your clothes!"

I walked up beside Jizo and said to him, "Can you do nothing about her?"

He shook his head, sadly. "It is Lord Emma-O's will that she be here. Whether he makes her do this as severe penance for sins in a former life or for some other reason I do not know. But I cannot interfere. It is saddest when she steals the clothes from the children. Or makes them pile rocks endlessly beside the river. Sometimes...sometimes when she is not watching, I will place rocks on the children's piles so that they can rest or travel on sooner. But that is all I can do. Let us go in."

We entered a long tunnel whose rocky walls and ceiling were covered with short stalactites, like teeth in an impossibly huge mouth. The souls of the dead were jammed in around us, but as my arms could pass through them, I did not feel pressed upon.

Down and down we walked until, at last, the tunnel entered a vast chamber filled with gray souls. At the far end, Lord Emma-O sat at a great black desk, set on a high dais. Horse-headed oni stood to either side of him, watching the crowd officiously. Emma-O looked as he had at Izumo—flickering, for he was still at Izumo part of the time, among other places. The high walls of the chamber had openings, and now and then Lord Emma-O would pause in his writing and point at a soul, who would go flying with a whoop or a wail through one of the holes in the walls.

"Follow close," said Jizo, and he pressed through the throng of gray personages right up to Lord Emma-O's dais.

"Jizo-san," said the Judge of the Dead, frowning. "What are

you doing here? Are you going to waste more of my time begging on behalf of yet another departed wretch?"

Jizo bowed politely and said, "No, O-sama. I do not come to speak on behalf of the dead."

"Good."

"I come on behalf of this one who is yet alive." Jizo stepped aside and gently urged me forward.

"You!" said Lord Emma-O.

"Begging my Lord's pardon," I said, bowing very low. "But you did invite me to appear and press my case, and so I have."

The Judge of the Dead looked back and forth between Jizo and me, scowling and chewing on a strand of his coarse beard. "Had I known you would bring him as your advocate, I would have reconsidered the invitation. Very well. Let us get this over with." He turned to one of the guardian oni, who handed him his two-headed staff. He pounded this on the dais three times and called out *"Chomigoto-san!"*

There was a crackle of lightning beside the dais, and the spirit of Lord Chomigoto appeared. He looked around wild-eyed and astonished. "What is the meaning of this, O-sama? You promised me I could haunt the Upper World as long as I chose!"

"Someone brings a charge against you, and you are called to answer it." Lord Emma-O pointed at me.

"You!" Lord Chomigoto shouted at me. He huffed and puffed so in his anger and surprise that I found it quite difficult not to laugh. I could see why the tengu called him Old Blowhard. "What are you doing here? Why aren't you in Tamba Province rebuilding my shrine?"

"It is that very matter," said Jizo mildly, "that we have come to discuss. Namely, have you the right to make such demands of this young girl?"

Lord Chomigoto's eyes went even wider, and he stepped back. "A bosatsu! Surely, Holy One, you must understand." He pointed at me. "She made the sacred promise, with sakaki leaves! She swore upon the kami of her clan!"

"As I understand it," said Jizo, "her promise was merely to repair the small shrine in which she had taken refuge. Nothing more."

"She is Nakatomi!" cried Lord Chomigoto. "They helped the Yamato usurp my throne! They owe me!"

"And what," said Jizo, "do *you* owe to the clan whom your people destroyed so that you could take the throne from *them*?"

Lord Chomigoto balled his fists. "That is different. They were weak. Unworthy."

Lord Emma-O thumped the floor of his dais with his staff. "That is also not relevant to the matter before us," he said. "Chomigoto-san, you are becoming an embarrassment to me. I begin to regret allowing you to return to the Upper World. I am beginning to consider dismissing the gimmu you have placed upon this girl."

I felt a smile begin inside me, but I did not let it reach my face.

"I must have my vengeance, O-sama!" shouted Lord Chomigoto. "At least let me curse the clan who plundered my tomb, Lord Tsubushima and his relatives."

The Judge of the Dead scratched his coarse beard thoughtfully. "There is some justice in what you suggest."

I began to nod in agreement, when I realized that the Tsubushima clan now included my sister. "No, O-sama!" I flung myself to the ground before his dais. "Or if you must allow it, please spare Tsubushima no Riko, for his wife is my sister Sōtōko, and she is blameless!"

"I cannot start allowing exceptions," said Lord Emma-O, "if he wishes to curse the entire clan."

"Then please, I beg you, do not allow him that curse!"

"How bothersome," sighed Lord Emma-O. "This matter is becoming complicated. You realize that if I relieve you of the gimmu, then we must deal with that other matter of your prior trespassing in my chamber uninvited."

Jizo looked sharply down at me. "You did not mention this. Is it true?"

"Yes. Forgive me," I said. "I did not wish to burden you with my past troubles. But, two years ago, I sought my eldest sister's husband's soul here. It is a long story."

"You see?" said Lord Chomigoto. "She is a liar as well as a promise breaker."

"Silence!" said Lord Emma-O. "You have had your turn to speak, Chomigoto-san. Now. How shall we untangle this knot, Jizo-bosatsu? What, in your opinion, is the wise and merciful thing?"

"Perhaps, my Lord," said Jizo, "we should hold Mitsuko-san to her promise after all, even as Lord Chomigoto has embellished it. To be merciful, however, let us bargain it down to two of the three demands, asking only that they need not be completed in a hurry. For any two of the three should be enough to occupy her, say, a lifetime?" He glanced toward the dais, and he and Lord Emma-O seemed to exchange a look of understanding.

I was distressed that my fate was being decided without anyone asking what I wanted. Had the admission of my trespassing turned Jizo against me? Yet I dared not speak up, lest I ruin what little chance for hope I had.

"That is a fair and wise compromise," said Lord Emma-O. "Which two do you suggest, Jizo?"

"Let us say the replenishment of the tomb and the gathering of the descendants of his worshipers." Jizo turned to Lord Chomigoto. "For those are the most difficult. Will that satisfy you?"

"Hmmm," said Lord Chomigoto. "Once my worshipers are gathered, they can build me a worthy shrine. Very well. I accept your compromise."

I stood up and shook the dust off the sleeves and skirts of my kimonos. I did not look at Jizo for fear I would burst into tears. "If you feel that is best," I murmured, "then I will also agree."

"Then let it be done!" proclaimed Lord Emma-O. He pounded the dais with his staff. "Chomigoto-san, you may return to your haunts."

The spirit of the wizard-king smiled at me, a most cruel and unpleasant smile. "I thank you, O-sama. Again your ruling shines as a testament to your eternal wisdom." The shade bowed deeply to the Judge of the Dead and then vanished.

"Jizo-bosatsu," said Lord Emma-O. "Return your charge to Heian Kyō, so that she may begin the task of satisfying the gimmu laid upon her. Swiftly. Her presence is disturbing."

Jizo-bosatsu bowed, as did I, and he gently began to lead me away from the dais. "Forgive me," he said softly. "I did not know about your prior...problem. To carry out his sentence for your transgression, Lord Emma-O would have had to end your life and claim your soul. I felt that by allowing you to take on the debt to Lord Chomigoto, you might yet at least have a long life. During that time, you might do enough holy work that I and other bosatsu could intercede again for you and keep you from O-sama's wrath. So shoulder your burden, but proceed slowly so that you may yet have time to save yourself."

Though his words did not cheer me, at least I now understood that Jizo had not turned against me but was doing his best to help me. "Ah. I see," I said. "Thank you."

Suddenly, the whole cavern began to shake, and a deep pounding rumble echoed all around us.

"Earthquake," I whispered, and I looked around wondering where I should run to.

Lord Emma-O's eyes glowed red. "*Susano-wo?*" he shouted.

"Ai yi yi yi yi yi yi yi!" High-pitched cries split the air, and black winged creatures spilled out of the holes in the walls and wheeled and dove in the air.

"The tengu!" I cried, astonished. "Why have they come?"

The tengu circled lower, and one of them had a girl on his back. It was Suzume! And she was throwing well-aimed pine-cones at the horse-headed oni. From her wide grin and shouts of glee, she seemed to be enjoying herself mightily.

A tengu landed beside me. "Mitsuko! Get on!"

"Goranu?"

"Who else, silly? We're rescuing you."

"But—"

"No buts. Get on!"

I looked at Jizo, but the bosatsu was trying to keep between me and two very angry oni. I gathered my kimonos and jumped onto Goranu's back.

"Ooof! You get heavier every time. Ai yi yi yi yi!" He leaped into the air with a mighty flapping of wings, and we flew down a low tunnel, narrowly missing a huge man with wild hair who was pounding on drums with great mallets. He nodded to us and winked at me as we passed.

"So you went to your Esteemed Ancestor, Susano-wo, after all!"

"Well, I had to, didn't I? I slipped into the conference at Izumo and made him feel guilty for getting you in trouble with Lord Emma-O."

"You were at Izumo?"

"I followed you and Kai-Lung there. You didn't think I was going to let you get into *too* much trouble, did you? What kind of a teacher do you think I am?"

The tunnel bent upward, and up, up we flew until we came out of a fissure in the earth. All the other tengu had followed behind us, a cloud of black birds erupting into the sky. The sun was beginning to rise, and the sky was filled with glorious shades of gold and purple. We flew over a mountain ridge, and there before us was the tengu village, a huge bonfire burning in the center.

We landed very near it, and there were tengu, male and female, dancing around the fire, singing and beating on little drums and striking little bells.

"Is this some sort of celebration?" I asked Goranu as I slid off his back.

"That's right!"

"For what?"

"You."

"Me?"

"You got Kai-Lung to fly you to Izumo."

"Well, yes, but—"

"You faced Old Blowhard and made a fool of him in front of Lord Emma-O!"

"Yes, but—"

"No buts! You have passed the test of Tengu-Do."

Someone came up behind me and put a cloak around my shoulders. It was made of black feathers.

Goranu walked up close to me, his eyes shining. "Mitsu-chan. I am so very proud of you." He placed his cheek against mine and, very briefly, put his arms around me and held me.

Then, laughing, he danced away, hooting and cavorting with the rest of the tengu around the bonfire.

Well. I sank to my knees, feeling very much as if I resembled my nickname.

> The icebound puddle
> now melts with the warmth of fires
> without and within.

I sighed as tears of joy ran down my face.

Desire

A plum tree in bloom
high on a steep cliff. My gaze
is captivated.

$\mathcal{I}$ A W O K E many hours later knowing that I had had the most wonderful dreams, though I could not remember them. It did not matter that I was waking up in a dilapidated tengu hut. Or that the first thing I saw was Suzume handing me a bowl of brown rice with bugs in it.

"I tried to pick most of them out for you," Suzume said, "but I'm sure I missed some. Do you want it anyway? Kuroihane told me this is what tengu eat for breakfast, but he might have been joking." I noticed she was even dressed like some of the tengu, black trousers and black hapi jacket.

I set the bowl aside, not feeling hungry. "Good morning. If it is morning. Do you know what hour it is?"

"No, but it's after noon. We're keeping tengu hours now, too, I see."

"So it would seem."

After a pause, Suzume said, "So. Did you sort everything out with Lord Emma-O?"

"Yes." I sighed. "In a way."

"So. I suppose you will be wanting to go home soon."

"Home?" For a moment I was disoriented. "Oh. You mean to Heian Kyō." I was suddenly reminded that I had another life, beyond tengu and dragons and the Lord of the Dead. I had a father waiting for me, and possibly a betrothal to an eleven-year-old prince. I had the obligations to Lord Chomigoto to discharge, as slowly as possible. I looked down at the rough floorboards of the tengu hut. "Yes, I suppose I must."

Suzume sat silently for many moments. Then she said, "Lady Puddle, I have something to ask. Would you...would you mind terribly if...would you permit it if...I did not return with you?"

"What? What are you saying?"

"I don't want to go back! I want to stay here, with the tengu!" She glared at me as if daring me to argue with her.

"Suzume," I said as gently as possible, "listen to how foolish you are being. We have no place here. These are not our people. Look how they live." I gestured at the primitive hut. "How can you wish to stay?"

"Of course you do not understand. You are used to being surrounded by nice things and behaving in stuffy ways. This place wouldn't suit you at all. But, don't you see, the tengu are so...happy. So wild and free. Tengu never worry about which kimono goes with which, or who is of what rank, or what kind of simpering poems to send to each other."

"But I thought you wanted to go to Court, Suzume."

She gazed out through the doorway. "I used to. Now that I have learned Tengu-Do, I see that all the finery and cultivated manners of you Good People is just foolishness."

I should have been insulted. Yet I could not be angry, for I understood. "It is not so much Tengu-Do, is it, but Kuroihane that makes you want to stay?"

"Well...well...and what's wrong with that?" she demanded.

"Suzume, haven't they told you? The...mixing of mortal and tengu is forbidden. They would never allow you to stay here."

Suzume balled her hands into fists and shut her eyes very tight as if to hold back tears. I reached over and put my hand on her arm. "I am sad to leave, too, Suzume. A part of me would like to stay. But it cannot be. You will forget Kuroihane in time. At Court you could easily find others to love—"

"Love!" Suzume snatched her arm away. "My mama told me about love at Court. Mama said a Court lady's serving-maid has to be careful because any nobleman who wants her can come creeping into a girl's chamber and...spend the night whether she wants him there or not. And if she acts unfriendly, things can go badly for her career."

"If she acts too friendly," I said, thinking of Kiwako, "it can be unfortunate, as well."

"There, you see? Trouble no matter what you do. What kind of love is that?"

"Well, then, you do not have to go to Court. You can stay at my father's house where you were—"

"You don't understand!" Suzume wailed. She jumped to her feet and glared down at me. "I see now. You are just jealous because you have to go back, even though you love Goranu. Just because *you* have family and obligations, you want me to go back, too."

"I am not jealous!" I exclaimed, though I feared she might be right. "Suzume, doesn't your family depend on the work you do? Are they not counting on you to do well in life and better their situation?"

"There! You see? All you can think of is nobility and rank and wealth. I don't want any of that. I want to stay here!"

I became very annoyed with her. "You are being childish," I said coldly. "This is a hopeless dream." As I spoke, I felt as though ice was again forming around my heart, for surely my dreams were as hopeless as hers.

Suzume defiantly stuck out her chin. "In our lessons in Tengu-Do, we were taught there is always a way around a problem. You may do as you please, but I will find a way to stay!" She flung the curtain aside and stomped out of the hut.

"Suzume!" Gathering my kimonos around me, I ran after her. In her haste, I saw her rudely knock aside Goranu, who was approaching the hut.

"Hey!" Goranu called after Suzume, but she did not stop or even look back.

I went up to him and bowed. "I am so sorry, Goranu. Forgive her, she is upset."

"And just what did you do to upset Kuroihane's ladylove so?"

"Oh," I said, my feelings decidedly mixed. "She is known as his ladylove now, is she?"

"Just teasing. Don't tell him I said that or he'll molt in embarrassment."

I gazed sidelong at Goranu, wondering if I was known by the other tengu as his ladylove or if I wanted to be, or if he would find it embarrassing. I wished my heart would stop being foolish like Suzume's. I had too many obligations—I could not dare to have such impossible hopes. I caught him looking at me, and I blushed and turned my face away.

"So," he went on. "What is the matter?"

"Eh?"

"With Suzume, silly girl. Why is she upset?"

"Oh. We were talking about going home. To Heian Kyō."

"Ah. I think I begin to see. I suppose you must. You have so much to do, after all."

"Yes." My spirits sank further, although I do not know what I was hoping he would say.

"However, you can't go just yet," he said cheerily. "You have to see your surprise."

"My surprise?"

"Yes! Look up." He pointed toward the sky.

I did and saw a line of tengu flying high above us, one after the other. The line stretched from the cloud-covered mountain nearby, where Kai-Lung lived, over the barrier cliffs that separated the tengu valley from the rest of the world.

"What are they doing?"

"Doing you a favor, since my cousins are as impressed as I am with your cleverness. And what a wonderful trick it is, too! Hee hee. You must come and see."

"A favor? A trick?"

Goranu spun around three times, changing into the form of a huge raven. "Jump on!" He cawed through his large beak when he had finished.

I noted that he was no longer shy about changing shape while I was watching, but I did not mention this to him. I clambered onto his back between his great black wings.

"Ooof!" Goranu said, as he always does, and he ran down the center of the tengu village, then leaped into the air with mighty beats of his wings.

I sighed and buried my face in his warm feathers, holding on tight. I wondered if this would be the last time I would ever fly on his back. I could scarcely bear the thought, and though I tried to stop them, my tears flowed. *Suzume might wish to stay in the tengu village. But if a great kami could grant my wishes, this is where I would wish to stay forever.* The hopelessness of such a dream overwhelmed me. I hoped that Goranu could not feel my tears through his feathers.

Alas, all too soon we set down again, in the forest clearing where the remains of the ruined shrine lay. The entrance to Lord Chomigoto's tomb was open. The clearing was filled with tengu, each carrying something into the tomb. Some brought swords with golden scabbards, some brought polished gems, and some brought bronze mirrors and pieced jade screens.

I slid off Goranu's back, horrified. "Oh no! What are they doing?"

"Replenishing Old Blowhard's tomb. That was part of your sentence, wasn't it? This was Kai-Lung's idea, actually. He said that after hearing your story, when he got back to his cave and saw all the things he had and didn't need, he decided to give them to your cause and rallied us to deliver it. What—you don't seem pleased. Are you being ungrateful again?"

"Oh, oh, forgive me, good Goranu. I am sure you all meant well—"

"Meant well? Hah! We are hoping Old Blowhard is churning in his grave like the waters of Lake Biwa on a windy day."

"Perhaps you meant kindness to me, then, but you do not understand." I nearly hopped up and down, my hands anxiously clasping and unclasping. "Jizo-bosatsu arranged that I still had to fulfill my debt for a reason. As soon as both parts of the gimmu are satisfied, I must answer to Lord Emma-O for my previous trespassing, which must mean my death. Your kindness has just brought me halfway closer to my doom!"

Goranu stared at me a moment, his beak gaping open. "Oh. Oh my." He spun around and around until he was in young-man form again. "Should I stop—no, I can't. Kai-Lung would be most offended if we returned his treasure to him. And my fellow tengu would have fits. Really, Mitsuko, you should have told me this sooner."

"Forgive me, Goranu, but you did not ask, and I did not think it would matter so."

"Yes, well, as the saying goes, we would all be wiser if we

lived backwards." Despite his joking manner, Goranu's face was pale and his brows furrowed with worry. "But you said you were halfway to your doom. What is the other half?"

"That I should gather the descendants of the villagers who lived here so that they might offer respects to Lord Chomigoto again."

"Oh!" Goranu exhaled a great sigh of relief. "Well. That should take forever, shouldn't it? Nothing to worry about. You're still safe."

"I suppose so." I stared down at my feet.

"Is she being ungrateful again, Highness?" asked Kuroihane, passing by with an armful of silk.

"On the contrary," said Goranu. "She is so overcome with gratitude, she cannot express herself."

"Heh," Kuroihane snorted, and he continued into the tomb.

Goranu looked down at me. "So, Mitsuko-san, what do you wish to do now?"

"I . . . I would like to go to my sister's house, since it is nearby. I should let her know that I am all right. Perhaps there I can think about what to say to my father when I get home."

"Very well. The way is not long. But it is getting late, and there are wild things in this forest. You should not go alone. May I walk with you?"

"Yes. Certainly."

With an expansive sweep of his arm and a bow, Goranu indicated the way out of the clearing and the path that led toward the Western Road. I followed him into the forest, leaving behind the clattering, chattering tengu filling Lord Chomigoto's tomb with Kai-Lung's treasure.

Goranu and I walked down the path in silence. The forest was very quiet except for the occasional birdcall and the padding of our feet on the ground. The air was cool and pleasant, scented with pine and flowers of the forest. There was no wind. The slanting sunbeams of the late afternoon turned the pine needles golden, and the world seemed to shimmer with a precious, magical light. I tried to let all of it seep into my memory, for I did not know if I would ever walk with Goranu beside me again. I wanted to remember what it was like, so that in future days of sorrow I could recall it to console myself.

"You are pensive," Goranu said at last. "You mortal girls are so moody. First Suzume nearly knocks me over, and now you won't even speak to me."

"Forgive me. She and I are both preoccupied with our cares," I said.

"Oh? What cares would the two of you share?"

I did not want to tell him my true thoughts. Being a tengu, he would probably just laugh at me. Or worse, be serious and tell me how foolish Suzume and I were. Or worse yet, I might again reawaken his hopes of learning the sutras to better his chance of meeting me as a mortal in a future life. So I said, "Neither Suzume nor I wish to go to Court."

"Ah, the Imperial Court," Goranu rhapsodized. "I haven't been there in a long while. I will admit it is a most impressive place. Why shouldn't you want to live there?"

I looked at him in surprise. "You mean you, a tengu, have been in the Imperial Palace? More than once?"

"Heh. We tengu visit the Court more often than mortals might care to think. So much opportunity to play delicious pranks there. That is where I first saw you—oh, I think I told you that. But it is so easy to slip in. There are so many bureaucrats running round, no one notices if there is one extra. Several highborn gentlemen there know me as Lord Atamasaru, Minister of the Yin-Yang Office of the Hour of the Monkey. Impressive title, neh?"

"But there is no such office, is there?"

"Of course not! But your Imperial bureaucracy is so huge and so constantly changing, nobody knows that. All I have to do is strut around in a black robe and a tall black hat, and I am treated with the greatest of courtesy, just in case I might be important. It's quite amusing, really."

"But... but if you can come to Court... then you could visit me there after I return to Heian Kyō, couldn't you?"

Goranu raised an eyebrow at me. "What, come to your pavilion when you are the number one wife of the boy-prince Komakai? Do you wish to cause a scandal, or do you just want me to see how happy you will be without me? Really, you can be quite cruel, Mitsuko-san."

"No! No!" I shoved my fists into my wide sleeves. "You do not understand. I will *not* be happy. I do not want to marry Prince Komakai! I want—" I pressed my sleeves against my mouth to keep my foolish words from spilling out.

"What is it you want?"

"I... I do not know."

"Hmmm. And Suzume? What does she want?"

"She said she wants to stay in the tengu village and live among you. That is impossible, of course, neh? But she has taken too much to heart what you taught us in Tengu-Do—that there is always a way around problems. She is determined to discover some way that a mortal may live among tengu."

"Is she?" mused Goranu. "Well. Suzume has certainly taken to tengu thought better than any mortal I have known. If anyone can solve that puzzle, it could be her."

Again, mad jealousy boiled up in me—that Suzume might do what I could not. I did not like to hear Goranu praise her so. But I said nothing for fear of what ugly words I might speak. Instead, I trudged in silence beside Goranu, feeling that the beauty of the afternoon had been quite ruined.

My footsteps slowed as I perceived through the trees ahead a clearing that would be the Western Road. I thought I could just make out a corner of the roof of Riko and Sōtōko's house. I tried to think what would be the proper way to say good-bye to Goranu.

"What if Suzume is right?" Goranu asked out of no-where.

"What? What do you mean?" I was irritated that he inter-rupted my thoughts to speak of her.

"What if there is a way that a tengu such as me and a mortal such as you can...remain in each other's company. Without learning painful sutras." Goranu stopped walking and gazed at me so intently that I blushed again. "If there is a way, would you want me to find it, too, Mitsu-chan?"

My breath caught in my throat. My conscience kept re-minding me of my father, of my duty to my clan and to my ancestors, and to all others who rely upon the power of the Fujiwara. But my heart spoke first. "Yes. Yes I would...Goru-chan."

A tiny smile curled his lips, and a light appeared within his eyes. "Then I will do my tengu-best to discover it. After all, I cannot let a mortal be better at Tengu-Do than I am, can I?"

I smiled back at him. "Of course not. That would be most embarrassing, neh?" We continued walking down the path, but my footsteps felt ever so much lighter.

"However," Goranu said, "if you should happen to use Tengu-Do to think of a way before I do, I will manage to forgive you somehow."

"I am glad to hear that." All too soon, only a few footsteps farther, I came to the edge of the Western Road. The gate to my sister's house was just beyond it. I blinked and realized, while I had been pleasantly distracted, I had not thought of a way to say good-bye.

"So. Here we are," Goranu said.

"Yes," I said, but I did not step onto the road. My feet did not want to move.

"How long will you be staying with your sister?"

"I do not know. A day or two, at least. I hope. I need time to think about what to tell my father. About...what to do."

"Yes. Good. Take your time. Time is good. For thinking. And things like that."

"Yes."

"Yes."

Quite suddenly he pulled me into his arms, and we held on to each other. We did not speak. It seemed we stayed that way for a long time, until the sun went behind the mountains. Perhaps it was only a minute or two, and I only wanted it to be forever.

But at last, Goranu pulled away from me. We did not say good-bye. He brushed his long nose against my cheek, and then, with a flurry of feathers, he was in bird form again and flapped his great black wings. I did not even shed a tear as I watched him soar high into the sky.

The mountain air, without the sun, turned chill, and at last I crossed the Western Road and knocked upon my sister's gate.

It was opened by the two guardsmen I had seen there before. As soon as they saw who I was, they pulled out their paper talismans, shouting, "The Tengu Lady!"

Calmly, I said to them, "If you please, I have returned and would like to see my sister Sōtōko at once."

"Yes! Yes! We will go tell her you are here immediately." They ran away from the gate as if I, myself, were a demon. It occurred to me, as I waited, that I had neither hid my face behind my sleeves nor bowed to deflect my gaze. I was becoming nearly as unsuitable for Court as Suzume.

Sōtōko came running down the wooden steps and into the garden. "Mitsuko! You are all right!" She hugged me and stepped back to look at me. "We were so worried about you. Riko sent a letter to Papa demanding that he call off the tengu at once."

"He sent a letter to Heian Kyō telling father I was here?"

"Yes. I could not dissuade him. Who knows what our father will think when he reads about you and the tengu, neh?"

"Who knows..." I murmured.

"But come in! This seems to be a night for guests arriving. There is someone else here whom I think you know."

"There is? Who?" I did not think I was ready for more surprises.

"Come in and see for yourself."

I followed my sister into her house, trying not to step on the fur rugs, when I saw a familiar face. "Dentō!"

The old ubasoku, wearing his usual gray robe and tiny box-like hat perched on his forehead, bowed, smiling. "Mitsuko-san. From what I have been hearing, your life has been as adventurous as ever. Your sister was just asking for my advice as to how to rescue you from the tengu. I told her that, given what I knew of you, it might be the tengu who have to be rescued."

I smiled awkwardly but did not know how to reply. Sōtoko set out cushions for us to sit on, and a servant brought tea and rice cakes. I spoke pleasantries to Sōtoko, reassuring her that I was well, that I had only been a guest in the tengu village for a time, and that they had not harmed me.

Sōtoko said, "That is good, for they certainly gave us a fright in the forest, neh?"

"They were just playing tricks," I said. "They would never have hurt you or Riko."

"And Riko? You should have seen his face, Mitsu-chan, he was so pale when he finally found me. And he babbled about your finding the shrine and how it would be impossible to fix and why we should forget the whole thing. When he saw you flying away with the tengu, I think he was almost relieved to see you go. Yesterday he rode off to his father's castle on some urgent business or other. He would not tell me what."

"I am so sorry he was frightened" was all I could say.

"Surely you cannot be blamed," said Sōtoko softly. She turned to idly watch the servants lighting the evening lamps.

I turned to Dentō and asked, "But how is it *you* come to

be here? When I spoke with you at Sukaku Temple, you were going to a distant village in order to cure a fever."

Dentō shook his head. "Alas, I arrived at the village too late to be of much use. The fever that afflicted the fishermen had passed on, and all I could do was say prayers for the dead and offer protective prayer-talismans to those who had survived it.

"As I was leaving the village, a cohort of Lord Tsubushima's men was passing by on the Tōkaido. Some of them recognized me and offered to let me travel with them for my safety and because they believe traveling with an ubasoku brings good luck. I stopped at Sukaku Temple, but you had already left for Heian Kyō. So I rode with the warriors all the way back here to Tamba Province. I remembered you had said that your sister now lived in this lodge, so I came here to ask if she had seen you."

"And now you can see me for yourself," I said.

"Yes." Dentō tilted his head to regard me from a different angle. "You have changed again. More serious changes this time."

"He is right," said Sōtoko, peering at my face. "I think you have become nearly half barbarian, as I am."

I did not answer, for surely they would have found the truth far worse.

An odd sort of wavering scream pierced the air, and Sōtoko sat bolt upright. A servant entered on her knees and bowed. "My Lady, your horse is restive in his stall and paces and kicks at his gate. We thought you might—"

"Yes, I will come at once," said Sōtoko, standing. "This is very odd," she said to me. "He is usually such a calm, gentle beast." She hurried off after the servant.

Dentō and I sat in awkward silence for some moments. At last, the old monk said, "Perhaps her horse hears or smells something that disturbs it. But tell me, has your effort to repair the shrine proceeded as you had hoped?"

I shook my head. "No, Dentō. It has all been...very strange. My father could not help me rebuild the shrine because he does not own the land it sits on. Lord Tsubushima, who owns the land, will not help me because...the shrine did not belong to any kami of stone or trees. It marked the tomb of an ancient Kofun priest-king named Lord Chomigoto. Whose tomb Lord Tsubushima's ancestors plundered many years ago."

Dentō gasped and rocked back on his heels. "Chomigoto! I have not heard that name since I was a child. Please. Go on."

"Well, because it took me two years to return to repair the shrine, his ghost appeared and made more demands of me: that I was to build him the grandest shrine the world had ever seen and replenish his tomb, which had been robbed by Lord Tsubushima's ancestors. And to find and gather the descendants of those who lived in a village by the shrine, so that Lord Chomigoto might be venerated again. By...various means, I again spoke with Lord Emma-O in his chambers because I felt Lord Chomigoto's demands were unfair."

Dentō gasped again, and his eyes went wide. "Such courage."

"I was aided in my claim by Jizo-bosatsu..."

"Jizo-bosatsu," whispered Dentō, awestruck. "You are truly traveling in exalted circles, Mitsuko-san."

"I suppose so," I said, blushing a little in embarrassment. "But because Lord Emma-O was still angry with me for trespassing in his chambers before, the demands were only reduced by one. Now Lord Chomigoto's worshipers will have to rebuild his shrine, but I still must replenish the tomb and gather the descendants of his worshipers."

"But I can help you, after all!" said Dentō. "At least with part of it—for I am the last living descendant of the villagers who lived near that shrine."

I felt suddenly cold all over, as if turned to ice. "You? You are—"

"Yes!" he nodded with enthusiasm. "The last. I remember now the stories my mother used to tell me. She managed to escape the slaughter of the other villagers by hiding. After being driven from the mountains, my mother earned her living as a traveling... well, never mind what. I was born in a wagon on the Tōkaidō. But she told me stories of how my father and the ancestors before him had served the shrine of a mighty king, whom they had to appease so that he would not curse them. It would seem that Chomigoto-sama was not a kind monarch, and it was rumored that he died from poisoning by one of his followers. My ancestors served him more out of fear than loyalty."

"But when I told you about the shrine," I said, still stunned, "why didn't you know that... that..."

"Who it belonged to? Because the way my mother had described it, I had thought Chomigoto's shrine was a big impressive structure, ornately carved and filled with fine things. As a young man, I returned to the mountains to search for the village and the shrine, but believed I had never found them. Indeed, I began to believe my mother had made up those stories. Had I known what you would find, Mitsuko-san, I would have warned you away from it or would have stayed by you to give more aid. But that is all clouds after the rain, one might say, for it would seem that, with me, your troubles are solved."

"No," I said softly. "They are not."

"What? Why, Mitsuko-san? Why do you look so sad?"

"Jizo-bosatsu arranged this debt so that I might have a lifetime to complete Lord Chomigoto's tasks. In this way, I might, over the years, do enough holy work to avoid Lord Emma-O's wrath when the time came for me to leave this world. But now the tengu have done me the favor of replenishing his tomb. And now you... you..."

"I have spared you the task of searching for his followers' descendants. Ah, Mitsuko, had I known. I am so very sorry. This is terrible. I had no idea—" Dentō stood, took a step toward me, then turned away, muttering, "There is always a way around trouble. There must be a way."

I glanced up at him, wondering why an ubasoku monk would quote a tenet of Tengu-Do.

But before I could ask, he prattled on. "Do not despair, Mitsuko-san. I will go meditate and pray, and perhaps between the two of us we can discover a solution. Yes. I will say nothing of this to your sister, never fear. Yes. Please excuse me." Dentō bowed and, anxiously muttering to himself, went away to a different part of the house to pray.

Sōtōko had left the shōji open when she left, and I stared out at the now dark and starry sky beyond it. I could see the tops of pine trees swaying in a silent breeze. I almost thought I could hear Lord Chomigoto uttering a hiss of satisfaction. But perhaps I just imagined it.

I sighed and turned my head away and stared at a lamp's flame dancing nearby. Watching it produced a state something like meditation, which was calming. *What does it matter,* I thought, *if I must now leave this world for Lord Emma-O's dungeons? I have already disappointed my family. I am bound up in foolish hopes and desires that will surely lead to nothing and only cause trouble. Very likely, my father believes me already dead. Very likely, Prince Komakai is betrothed to someone else. What does it matter if I must soon be taken from this Land of Illusion?*

It mattered to me, I realized. There would be so much I would miss. Who knows what karmic burdens another turn on the Wheel of Rebirth would bring? I was just getting used to the burdens of this life. And its joys. I would miss my sisters and brother. I would even miss Suzume. And Goranu. More than anyone, Goranu.

"I do not think Tengu-Do can find a way around this problem," I murmured. "It is harder even than mortals living among tengu. There is no way to leave one's life and yet stay." Tears blurred my vision, distorting the shapes in the lamp's flame. I saw in the new patterns the woman from my dreams. She was dancing and shaking sakaki branches, as always. Then she turned, and I saw her face. And I knew who she was. She was me.

I gasped and fell back against the floor cushions. *Blessed Amida, what is the meaning of this vision?* I wondered. *How can I—* And then it struck me, all at once, what it meant and what I must do. I jumped up and ran to where Dentō sat, chanting his prayers.

Attachment

A spiny seed has
stuck itself onto my sleeve.
Where should I take it?

"Dentō!" I cried.

He looked up from the pile of herbs he was burning in a brazier. "Yes? Mitsuko-san, what is it?"

"I think I have the answer. I know what I can do to avoid Lord Emma-O's judgment. But I need your help."

"Do you? Please tell me how I can assist you."

"I have just had a vision. I saw the woman dancing with sakaki branches again. But when I saw her face, it was me!"

"Was it?" said Dentō. "And what do you think this means?"

"Please, Dentō-san." I flung myself to the floor prostrate before him. "Please take me as your acolyte. Make me an uba-soku, as you are!"

"Well," Dentō murmured, fingering his wispy white beard. "Well, this is an interesting turn to things."

"You told me the women of my clan, when we were Nakatomi, could become ubasoku. You said you thought I, perhaps, had the same abilities they did. Won't you please teach me?"

"I...I would be honored to have so noble an acolyte to teach, Mitsuko-san. But I confess I do not see how this will help you in your troubles with Lord Emma-O."

"The Judge of the Dead told me that as punishment for my trespassing, he would have to end my life. But an ubasoku, just like any other monk or nun, must cut all ties to his previous life, neh? He must change his name, and cut his hair, and live separate from human activity, neh? Is that not like dying?"

"Well, yes, in a manner of speaking—"

"Then, perhaps, I can bargain with Lord Emma-O. Perhaps he will accept an ending to my present existence. Fujiwara no Mitsuko will no longer be, and I shall become a new person, completely different from what I ever was. Do you think he might accept this?"

"Bargain with the Judge of the Dead?" whispered Dentō in wonderment. "Avoiding your trouble by becoming someone else? What has made you capable of such unusual thoughts, Mitsuko-san?"

"Please do not think ill of me for this," I said. "But Goranu has been teaching me Tengu-Do. It is he—and a rice cake girl named Suzume—who has prepared me for such thinking."

"Indeed?" sighed Dentō. "How extraordinary. It must be fated that you become an ubasoku. For I will tell you something very few people know. Many ubasoku receive training from tengu. That is where we get some of our...unusual abilities. Even I had such training, long ago."

I sat up. "You did?" So that is how he knew the tengu teaching that there is always a way around trouble. "But I thought you were suspicious of tengu, and you did not even recognize Goranu when you first met him."

Dentō smiled. "It is always wise for a mortal to be wary of tengu, particularly a monk like me. They are always up to tricks, no matter how friendly they seem. I had never seen your friend Goranu before. I only got to know one of them well: my tengu-sensei, whose name was Kuroihane."

"Kuroihane! I have met him."

"Have you? I see him at a distance in the forest from time to time, but we have not spoken in many years."

"But if tengu hate monks and monks are suspicious of tengu, how can this association be?"

Dentō crushed an aromatic leaf between his fingers and let the crumbs fall into the brazier. "An agreement was made long ago when the first ubasoku came to these mountains. The tengu permitted the ubasoku to remain if the ubasoku promised not to drive out or try to preach to the tengu. In return, the tengu would share some of their knowledge and keep away monks and priests of competing sects. It has not always been successful, for the tengu cannot help what they are, but there is a sort of peace between us."

I thought this over for some moments. "Then, my friendship with Goranu is no barrier to my becoming your acolyte?"

"Not at all. But you must consider well," said Dentō with a frown, "the consequences of your actions. You will not be marrying Prince Komakai, and therefore your family, the Fujiwara, may lose prestige."

"I am aware of this," I said softly, "but that would be true if Lord Emma-O takes my life, as well. It cannot be helped. Perhaps as an ubasoku I can use my powers and prayers to prevent greater misfortune from falling on my family."

Dentō nodded thoughtfully. "Yes, this is possible. I am glad you have given it thought. Well, then. What must we do? I have not yet presented myself to Lord Chomigoto's shrine, so we may have a little time to prepare. It was Jizo-bosatsu who was your advocate to Lord Emma-O, you said? How did this happen?"

"He was summoned for me by the saintly spirits beyond the Great River. Is there a temple nearby at which I might ask the monks to send prayers to Jizo-bosatsu?"

Dentō scratched his wispy beard. "There is no Buddhist temple within miles of here, Mitsuko-san. However, I know a place not far away where there are many stone images of bo-satsu. I believe his is among them. Perhaps if I do an offering and invocation there, we might get Jizo's attention."

I fidgeted with my hands. "Then I suppose that is what we must do. We should leave right away, neh?"

"No, no, Mitsuko-san. Travel at night through a haunted forest? That is hardly sensible. No, we must wait until morning. Have patience, Mitsuko-san. Lord Emma-O can surely wait a few hours more, and so can you." It was clear Dentō would not change his mind. I had no choice but to trust him.

When Sōtōko returned from calming her horse, I told her nothing about my decision. I said only that I was tired and was ready to sleep. She led me to a room where I could curl up on a soft reed mat. It took me a while to get to sleep, for I feared being pounced on by Lord Emma-O's demons. But eventually I drifted off to slumber, with no dreams, and was woken up at dawn by Sōtōko shaking my shoulder.

She gave me warm broth and rice for breakfast, and told me Dentō was already awake and meditating in the garden. "So what will you do now?" she asked as I ate. "Do you still plan to somehow repair the shrine?"

I did not know what I dare reveal—surely, Tsubushima no Riko did not want the shame of his clan talked about, or for me to frighten Sōtōko with tales of a ghost nearby or to worry her with my plans to become an ubasoku. So I merely shrugged and said, "I must think about it."

"Since it is no longer a simple matter, can you not let Papa worry about it and return home?"

"No, I cannot return home yet."

"Couldn't your magical tengu build a new shrine for you?" Sōtōko asked with a frown.

"They have the power, but they wouldn't. They told me they will have nothing to do with shrines."

"What good are they, then? They are ugly and mean, and they use their magic only for tricks. I cannot understand why Father permits you to associate with them."

I wanted to explain but dared not let her know my feelings about Goranu. She would doubtless be horrified. "They helped our family escape from Lord Tsubushima's castle, remember?"

Sōtōko looked away. "Yes, I suppose there is that. So. What are you going to do?" she persisted. "Are you going to fly on a tengu back to Heian Kyō?"

"Ummm..." I found I could not tell her about my decision to become an ubasoku. What if she tried to stop me? What would she tell our father? It hurt to have to avoid the truth so much with her. "Dentō and I are going to a nearby stone bosatsu to, umm, pray for inspiration on the matter."

Sōtōko's frown deepened. "By yourselves? I can have my two guardsmen accompany you. They are not very smart, but they might frighten away any bears or brigands."

"No!" I said, too quickly. "I mean, we are not going far. You should not trouble your household on our account."

Sōtōko looked down at the floor, her mouth set in a thin line. "Mitsu-chan. If you are in some sort of trouble, I wish you would confide in me. That is what family is for, neh? I would give you whatever assistance I can."

"Sōtō-chan," I began, but my voice caught in my throat. It was very hard to keep from bursting into tears. "If there was anything—anything you could help with, I would tell you."

"I see" was all she replied.

Just then, Dentō walked in. "Ho, you are awake now, Lady Mitsuko! Very good. Are you ready for our walk?"

I stood, guiltily glad for the excuse to leave Sōtōko's company. "I am, Dentō-san." I bowed and smiled.

"Then let us be on our way."

Sōtōko saw us to the gate in silence, still upset that I was keeping secrets from her. I did not know what to say to reassure her, so I simply tried to appear as calm and happy as I could.

Dentō and I walked up the road, northward toward Lord Tsubushima's castle, for a ways. Then Dentō pointed out a small path branching off to our left into the forest, and we took it. I had a difficult time keeping up with him, for Dentō was used to walking great distances nearly every day, whereas I had only recently had to walk much at all. I was huffing and puffing so much, I did not try to converse with him. But once we entered the forest, he slowed down a bit, and I could catch my breath. And I could ask him about something important.

"Dentō-san, since you were trained by them, you must know a lot about tengu, neh?"

"I know some things. Although, by now, perhaps you know more than I do. Why?"

"Well, it seems . . . I have a servant who has become . . . quite taken with the tengu. She wants to stay with them and . . . and possibly even marry one of them. But . . . I have heard that such a thing is forbidden."

Dentō began to laugh, and I could no longer doubt that he had been trained by tengu. "Ho, ho, ho, you are right, and for good reason! You have a foolish servant indeed. Tengu and mortals are quite different creatures. Any offspring from such a marriage would be very strange, and quite miserable, I am sure. Such a child would have powers that would frighten any mortal community, yet it would not be able to do all the things a tengu can do. Such a creature would be unwelcome in either world. And then there are the theological matters to consider—far too confusing. No, it is wise that the tengu stay as apart from us as they do. You should discourage this servant, if you can. Her hopes are quite ridiculous."

"I see," I said, feeling quite discouraged myself. My hopes of the evening before seemed to vanish like smoke. Was Goranu simply foolish, too? But what was the point of even thinking about it?

> Hopes and plum blossoms,
> so delightful to hold
> but oh, how fragile...

I noticed that Dentō gave me one wondering glance over his shoulder, but he said nothing more.

As we walked, clouds gathered in the sky. At first there were only a few. But they billowed larger and darker. For a while, I thought it was only my mood that made the weather seem angry and unsettled. But the clouds continued to gather overhead until the sky grew so black that I feared a great storm was upon us. Yet, though a chill storm wind blew, no rain fell, and there was no dampness in the air. I began to feel uneasy. "Dentō—these clouds..."

"Yes. The mountains can produce strange storms, yet this does not seem natural. No matter, we are almost there."

After a few minutes more of walking, a clearing opened up before us. But it was not a pleasant meadow or mountain lake. It was an area of nearly bare earth—only scraggly weeds growing over it. Large stones stuck out of the ground like bits of dragon bone. "What is this place?"

"It is where the village that Tsubushima's ancestors destroyed once stood. I do not, as a rule, come here, for it is an ill-aspected place."

"Lord Chomigoto's village? We are not near his tomb, are we?"

"Not near, no. But we are not far. Other ubasoku have tried

to offer prayers here in the past and put up images of bosatsu in hopes that the sight of saintly ones might ease the suffering of the unquiet dead."

"Unquiet dead," I whispered, pulling my kimonos tighter around me. Something tugged at my sleeves and hair, but when I turned I saw nothing. Only wisps of white out of the corners of my eyes. "Dentō—"

"Let us hurry. Over here."

I followed him, trying to calm myself. Had I not stood before the Lord of Death? What had I to fear from spirits? Spirits had helped me when I stood at the River, even summoning Jizo for me. But those had been saintly souls, not tormented wraiths unable to leave this world. Stories of ghosts possessing the bodies of the living came to mind, spirits who could freeze one's blood just by looking at one. I hurried up to Dentō, who was kneeling by some fallen stones.

I knelt down beside him as he picked up one of the stones. It was a crude statue of Jizo, very simplified. Dentō placed it on a flat rock and began to lay out little braziers.

The wind plucked at my kimonos again, and I turned to look behind me. Pale faces of women and children, but distorted, mouths open and eyes wide, stared back at me. "Dentō!" I whispered urgently, "There are ghosts—"

"Pay them no mind!" he said. "I must concentrate on the summoning. Give me some strands of your hair."

"My hair?"

"You will be cutting much of it when you become my acolyte, neh? What are a few strands to you now?" Dentō pulled from his brown pouch a short, sharp knife and cut a few strands of my hair. He blew on the tiny coals in the brazier and laid the hair across them. The smell this produced was not pleasant.

Dull thunder rumbled in the sky, but I did not turn around.

Dentō threw some sandalwood chips into the brazier as well, changing the scent, though not making it sweeter. Then, clasping his hands together, he rocked back and forth, chanting as the saintly souls had done, "Jizo, Jizo, Jizo, Jizo—"

I did not know whether I should join in, but I did to distract myself from the pale presences behind me. My spine felt cold, as if someone were trickling ice water down my back.

A golden glow appeared around the crude statuette. Although the stone image did not change, a voice spoke out of the air above it. "Who is it who so urgently summons me, in so dire a place?"

"Jizo!" I cried.

"I pray on behalf of one you have helped before, O Holy One," said Dentō, bowing until his forehead touched the ground.

"Ah!" the voice continued. "Fujiwara no Mitsuko. I had not expected to speak with you again so soon. What would you ask of me?"

"Jizo-bosatsu," I said, "I have unintentionally fulfilled the terms of my sentence. My tengu friends have replenished Lord Chomigoto's tomb with the treasure of the dragon Kai-Lung. And the one who summoned you is the last descendant of Chomigoto-sama's worshipers."

"Ah. Ah. Who would have guessed that such extraordinary friends could do such harm? But that is tengu for you, neh? I am so sorry for you, Mitsuko-san. I did what I could."

"You are blameless, Jizo-bosatsu. But, if you please, there is one more thing you may do for me. I have an offer to make to Lord Emma-O regarding my crime of trespassing in his realm."

"An offer? You must understand, Mitsuko-san, that O-sama takes his justice seriously. He is not to be trifled with."

I pulled my kimonos closer around me as the wind began to blow harder. "I understand. I am serious, I promise you."

"It must be equal to what he had intended, which is to take your life from you."

I felt thoroughly cold, inside and outside. "Just so. Would he be satisfied if Fujiwara no Mitsuko ceased to exist? If I become the acolyte of this ubasoku who summoned you, change my name, and cut all ties to my former existence?"

"Ah. I see. That is an interesting solution. Indeed, it may. I would have to argue it carefully...yes. I will present your offer to O-sama. But if he agrees, you must be prepared to make this change soon."

"I am ready to do so, as soon as I hear he has accepted it."

"Good. Your willingness to quickly comply should make him think better of your offer. I will go to him this very moment. I will let you know what he decides."

"Thank you, Jizo-bosatsu!" I bowed low to the little statue.

There was no further reply, and the golden glow disappeared from around the statue.

I stood and realized that the presence of the bosatsu had kept the ghosts at bay. But now they reappeared—a white face baring long teeth was suddenly right in front of me. Something touched my arm, and painful cold seeped into my skin, turning to ice in my bones. I feared the spirit was going to slip inside me like a knife and possess me.

"Be gone!" said the ghost.

"Leave this place!" said another.

"Never return!" said yet a third.

"Dentō!" I screamed, unable to move.

The old monk left his brazier and came up beside me. He blew some powder at the ghosts. "By the kami of this forest," he cried at them, "I command you to disperse!"

The ghosts jerked back a short distance but did not flee. "Heed us!" said the first one. "Do not remain!"

Lightning crackled overhead. I do not think it was normal lightning, for I have never seen bolts such a color of green before. My long hair stood on end and whipped about me as though it were alive.

Dentō grabbed my sleeve and pulled me toward the forest path. "There is more than ghosts in this. I have never seen such a storm before."

I found I could move again, and I gladly ran with Dentō away from the clearing and its unhappy spirits. "What do you think might be causing this? Did our summoning of Jizo make it worse?"

"Surely not. But I wonder if Lord Chomigoto is up to something."

"The tengu said all he could do was command the winds, bring bad dreams, and curse people."

"The tengu may not know everything."

We ran and ran down the forest path, the boughs of the pines thrashing at us as though the trees meant to knock us down. Fortunately the path led downhill, or I am sure I would have collapsed from exhaustion. Dentō kept looking to the south and west where Lord Chomigoto's tomb lay, as if expecting to see proof of his fears. I hoped the tengu of the forest were somewhere safe. I hoped Dentō and I would be somewhere safe soon. The wind was terrifying and now and then pushed me from the path into the grasping boughs of the pines. However, no rain fell upon us, and the lightning did not strike near us.

When we finally stopped to catch our breath, I asked Dentō, "Why were the spirits so angry with us? Were we disturbing them by summoning Jizo over their burial place? The spirits in the Land of the Dead also were disturbed by my being there, but surely it is not the same in this world."

"I do not think," said Dentō, huffing and puffing, "that the spirits were angry. I think they were warning us. I think they know what is happening. If they were formerly vassals of Lord Chomigoto, they may understand what he can do."

"Then perhaps we should not have run so soon. We should have stayed and asked them what we should beware of."

Dentō shook his head. "If they had wanted to tell us, they would have. Perhaps they are constrained in some way."

"But why," I said with some fear, "should Lord Chomigoto be angry? He is getting what he wants, neh?"

"He may somehow know you are trying to avoid Lord Emma-O's judgment. You told me he wished vengeance against the Nakatomi, and that may be more important to him than the grave goods or the shrine. Come, let us hurry to your sister's house before he decides to do more than buffet us with his wind."

I was not certain we were doing the best thing, for I did not wish to bring danger to Sōtōko. But I had no wish to argue with Dentō and did not know what else to suggest.

The sky was so dark with clouds by the time we reached the gate of Sōtōko's house that I no longer knew the time of day. I was nearly faint with exhaustion, such that I could barely stand. Dentō pounded on the gate, but the guards would not open it.

"Stay out, mountain wizard!" they cried. "Bring no more bad fortune to this house!"

"Bad fortune?" I gasped.

"Alas, among some people, ubasoku have as bad a reputation as tengu. You must remember this if you wish to become like me."

After we both did much pounding on the gate and shouting, at last Sōtōko met us at the gate herself. "Come in! Come in! Hurry! I will have Riko dismiss those awful guardsmen as soon as he returns."

We ran up the steps and into the main house as a great bolt of lightning flashed above us and thunder rolled louder than the lashing of Kai-Lung's tail. In its bright light, I thought I saw a dark shape on the veranda. I blinked, and it was gone.

Sōtōko guided us to the centermost room of the house,

where there was the best protection against the wind. The lodge was so drafty, one could not keep all of the breezes out, so the servants were constantly relighting the lamps. Sōtōko had cushions put out for us and served us warm broth. She seemed to be carefully not asking any questions.

A servant rushed in and bowed low. "Great Lady, there is an Imperial courtier on the veranda! He begs you to give him shelter from the storm!"

"A nobleman? Let me see this personage." Sōtōko hurried after the servant.

A thousand fears descended on me. Could Lord Chomigoto have arrived to threaten me and my sister? Perhaps Lord Tsubushima is here, angry that I have caused his family's shame to be revealed. What if my father has come all the way from Heian Kyō to take me back? The storm had upset me so, I could not imagine this visitation could bode well.

Sōtōko returned, followed by a courtly gentleman in the billowing black robes and tall hat of the First Rank. He was pleasant in appearance, but I did not recognize him. "I thank you, Kind Lady, for your hospitality," he was saying to Sōtōko in a bland and cultured voice. "I fear I have become separated from my retinue, and my horse was frightened by the lightning and threw me. I am most glad your house was here and you proved to be so kind to a stranger."

"I am glad this lowly house may receive and shelter so eminent a visitor," said Sōtōko. "Please excuse our rough furnishings and manners. This is but a simple mountain lodge, and my husband and I are not of great wealth."

"It is no matter," said the gentleman. "I do not expect to find the Golden Pavilion everywhere I travel." He looked at me, and I was suddenly quite aware that I was not behind a kichō. Belatedly, I held my sleeves up in front of my face. There was amusement in his eyes at that, which seemed somehow familiar.

Dentō tilted his head and regarded the gentleman with curiosity, but said nothing.

"If I may ask, what brings you all this way, Most Noble Lord?" asked Sōtōko.

"I have come up the Western Road on what may be a foolish chase, I fear," said the gentleman. "I come urgently seeking a noble girl, Fujiwara no Mitsuko by name. I was told she might be in this region. I have an important message for her."

My heart nearly stopped. *So he has come from Father after all. What will I tell him?* I fervently hoped that Sōtōko would not point me out, but of course she could not know that I wished such a thing.

Sōtōko smiled. "Why, good fortune smiles upon you, Noble Sir. The lady you seek is my own sister, and there she sits. Your search was not so foolish after all."

"Indeed? How wondrous! A helpful kami must have guided me here." He turned to me and inclined his head. "Great Lady Mitsuko, I am glad to have found you. I am Lord Atamasaru, of the Yin-Yang Office of the Hour of the Monkey. I bring news from the Court, which you will doubtless find interesting."

I coughed, then, into my sleeves to keep myself from laughing with joy and relief, for I now knew who he was.

Sōtōko frowned at me with concern, "I am sorry, Mitsuko, are you uncomfortable? Shall I get you a curtain of modesty?"

"Please do not trouble yourself," I replied. "I am sure the good gentleman understands the circumstances. What news does the Esteemed Lord of the Monkey bring?"

Sōtōko stared, somewhat scandalized.

The black-robed gentleman slid gracefully to his knees before me and said, "I bring news of your family, some of which may be pleasing to you and some of which may not. Your father has isolated himself in mourning concerning your disappearance, though he continues to hire men to search for you."

Sōtōko asked, "Did he not receive my letter? We told him she was with us."

"As to that, I cannot say," replied the gentleman. "But to continue. Naturally the planned meeting and betrothal between you and Prince Komakai was not possible. However, it may interest you to know that there is another Fujiwara who has caught the prince's eye, whom it would serve your family well to send in your stead."

"Oh?" I said. "Who might this be?"

"As it happens, the charming Fujiwara no Kiwako has enticed his interest."

"Kiwako!" Sōtōko and I cried in unison.

"But she suffers from a...questionable reputation," I said.

"So it is said," the gentleman murmured, "and that is why the young prince finds her interesting."

Again, I had to stifle my laughter. "I will admit this is pleasant to hear, Good Sir," I said. "But surely you did not come all this way simply to amuse me?" Although, considering his tengu nature, perhaps he had.

The gentleman turned to Sōtōko and said, "If you please, Good Hostess, I would like some plum wine. And a dish of grated daikon and carrot, if it is possible."

Sōtōko said, "I regret that our house is ill-prepared for visitors. We may not have such things."

"Will you do me the kindness of going to look? I do find I am quite thirsty."

Sōtōko was clearly aware she was being dismissed from our presence, and in her own house, but because it was a nobleman of the First Rank asking, she could not say no. I realized then how strange the manners of Good People are, and how based on illusion. Particularly in this instance, for the gentleman was not really a gentleman at all.

Reluctantly, Sōtōko bowed and left the room.

The nobleman eyed Dentō a moment but did not ask the ubasoku to leave. A few moments after Sōtōko had gone, the gentleman—in a very Goranu-like gesture—leaned forward, elbows on floor and head in hands. "Well, Little Puddle, I thought that, since you have an interest in maintaining the fortunes of your family, you might have use for this news. You can set up Kiwako in your place so you don't have to marry a boy-child. The only problem is, your father and other relatives don't quite trust her and so aren't yet willing to present her formally to the prince. If we can think of a way to convince them to do so, the Fujiwara fortunes may yet be preserved, and you will be free of that idiotic obligation."

I smiled sadly at him and said, "I thank you for this information, Noble Sir, but I regret there is little I can do. Very soon, if all goes well, I will be a Fujiwara no longer."

"What?" He sat bolt upright, Goranu-nature shining through his astonishment. "You are not going to marry someone else, are you?"

"You misunderstand, sir," I said patiently. "I once was taught that sometimes to avoid trouble one must become a different person. I fear this now applies very well to my situation."

The gentleman rubbed his face, eyes wide with uncertainty. "Surely the person who taught you that did not mean you should change permanently."

"Perhaps not, but I fear that is what is required."

The gentleman got up and started to pace the room. It seemed that black feathers were beginning to sprout from his robe. "Why? And what manner of change is this?"

I did not know if I should continue speaking circumspectly, for I did not know if Sōtōko might be listening. I decided it would be too difficult, so I stated things directly. "As it happens, both strictures of my debt to Lord Emma-O are now fulfilled. Lord Chomigoto's tomb is replenished, and the last surviving descendant of his village has been found." I indicated Dentō, who had been sitting in silence all this time.

"You!" Goranu turned and glared accusatorily at the monk.

Dentō shrugged. "Alas, Noble Sir, I did not know the nature of her debt when I revealed my parentage. It appears my very existence spells the noble Mitsuko's doom. The only way to save her is to take her on as my acolyte and teach her to be an ubasoku, so that she may cut all ties to her previous existence and be Fujiwara no Mitsuko no more."

"Jizo-bosatsu," I explained, "is presenting my offer to Lord Emma-O, and it is my hope that the Lord of Death will accept."

Goranu scratched his chin. His nose seemed to be growing longer. "Well. I see. Well. I suppose you had no choice, then. Change or die. So. Going to become an ubasoku, are you?"

"That is my hope," I said. I gazed down at the patterns on the reed mat beneath me. "It is the only hope I have left."

"Well," Goranu said, returning to pacing back and forth. His sandals seemed to be sprouting talons. "I see. No more Fujiwara no Mitsuko. Well. But that is all right. Perhaps all is not lost. Every ubasoku needs a tengu teacher, neh?"

"So I have heard," I said.

"And it takes years of training before an ubasoku becomes a full monk or nun, taking on all the strictures, neh?" His voice had become a caw, for his mouth and nose were now nearly a beak.

"So it does," said Dentō, with a wry smile.

"Then, then . . . at least, I can still be near you. As a teacher, that is. For a while." The robes on his back fluttered and became great black wings.

"For a while, perhaps," I said, though I truly did not know if I should encourage his hopes. And mine.

"Then, perhaps," Goranu went on, "there will still be time. Time to consider other . . . things. You know."

"So there may," I said, though it tore at my heart to think I might be lying.

Sōtōko bustled in carrying a tray with a cup, a bowl, and a small ceramic bottle. "Ai!" she exclaimed upon seeing Goranu, and she dropped the tray with a crash.

"What is the matter with you, woman?" cawed Goranu.

"A tengu!" Sōtōko cried. She turned to Dentō. "Can you not shoo it away? What has he done with our noble guest?"

"Why, as it happens, this is our noble guest," Dentō said mildly. "If I am not mistaken, this is Goranu, prince of the tengu in this region. And the information he has brought us may be of great service to Lady Mitsuko. I see no reason to rudely chase him from our company."

"It is all right, Sōtōko," I said. "I know this one well. He will do no mischief here."

"Tempting as it might be," added Goranu.

"Stop it," I said, but gently.

"But she has wasted good plum wine!"

"I . . . I will get you another cup. Highness," said Sōtōko, and she ran from the room.

"I wager we won't see her again this evening," muttered Goranu.

"Goranu-san," I said. "I thank you for trying to help, and I wish there were something I could do for Kiwako and my family, but my life—if I will still have one—will be following a different path. One that requires I cut myself off from the world I knew."

"Not necessarily," said Dentō. "There is a possible good use for the information your friend has been so diligent to bring us. You may yet be able to save your family's fortunes, even after giving up your family name. In fact, especially so, and especially if you begin training as an ubasoku."

"But as my teacher, shouldn't you advise me to forget my family's troubles?"

"I cannot expect my student to properly concentrate upon her studies if she is full of guilt and worry about her relatives. Besides, if you agree to what I have in mind, we may consider it a test of your willingness and determination to enter the sort of life I live. For it will require great concentration and restraint upon your part."

"How? What must I do?" I asked.

Dentō described his idea, and when he had finished, Goranu said, "That is extremely clever. Are you sure, old man, that you were not a tengu in a previous life?"

"As certain as you are," Dentō replied, "that you were not once a monk."

"Pah!"

To forestall an argument, I said, "Listen! It would seem the strange storm outside has stopped."

"I guess Old Blowhard has finished celebrating his victory," grumbled Goranu.

"I think," said Dentō, "that the storm was not celebration but the work of a sorcerer who is testing his powers. Not the sort of thing a spirit who is contemplating final rest might do."

"What do your fellow tengu say?" I asked Goranu.

"How would I know? I've been away at Court. I haven't seen any of them lately."

Suddenly, the ceiling glowed with a golden light, and Jizo, resplendent in his red cape, stepped down through the air.

"Ai!" cried Goranu. "A bosatsu!" He ran to a far corner of the room and cowered underneath a wing. Dentō and I bowed before the bosatsu as he stepped onto the floor.

"Peace, I bring you good news," said Jizo in his beautiful voice. "Lord Emma-O has accepted your offer, provided you begin the change immediately. He asks only that you never again enter his chambers until it is your proper time to do so. That applies to your demon friends, as well." Jizo cast Goranu a sly glance. "Farewell. All blessings be upon you," he said, and ascended back through the ceiling. I watched him go with torn heart, for there was another question I would ask but dared not while others were present. Too quickly, the golden glow vanished.

At last I turned toward Goranu, who still huddled under his wing. I had to keep from laughing at him as I said, "It is all right, Goranu. He is gone."

"You wouldn't be so amused," Goranu grumbled as he unfolded himself, "if *your* skin itched intensely whenever one of them was near."

"I suppose not," I said. "Forgive me."

"Begging your pardon, Mitsuko-who-is-to-be-Mitsuko-no-more," said Dentō. "But we now have much to do in order to obey O-sama's order. And it must be done without observers," he added, looking at the tengu.

"Yes, of course," I said, feeling sadness fall upon me like a dark shadow. "May I at least...say good-bye to him?"

Dentō nodded solemnly.

Both Goranu and I stood, and we walked together out to the veranda. We did not touch one another.

The sky was clearing, revealing bright afternoon sunlight. Birds sang cheerfully in the pine boughs. It felt all wrong with my mood, and I wondered if the kami were laughing at me. I could not look at Goranu beside me.

He pretended to be dusting off his feathers. "Your sensei is right, you know. It is better that I go. All that chanting would give me a headache."

"Yes. Surely."

"You know, it does not matter whether your name is Mitsuko. A person is not a name. It only means fourth child, anyway—why should you be just a number?"

"Yes."

"It doesn't matter that you won't be Fujiwara either. Rank is not important to a tengu."

"Yes." I had to hold my hands to my mouth. I wished he would stop talking, for I feared a flood of tears would burst from me any moment. Yet I also wished he would stay and talk forever.

"It doesn't matter that you have to cut your hair—"

"Goranu!" I could stand it no longer and began to weep.

"Oh, so, so, stop that now. I'm sorry. I've made you cry again. Please, pay me no mind. I am just a silly tengu, after all."

"No," I moaned into my hands. "You are not just that. Or I would not cry."

He did not respond for long moments. "It seems the whole world stands between us, neh?" he said softly, at last. "Or we can be as close as a boat and a riverbed...able to see one another but never...together. I do not know if I should hope anymore. Or what I should hope for. I do not know even if it would be kind to be near you. I might keep you from finding the Heavenward Path, after all."

I could hardly speak, for my sorrow. "I do not think...life of any sort would be worthwhile...if I thought that...I would never see you again."

"Well." He sighed loudly and said again, "Well. We cannot have Lord Emma-O get you into his clutches again so soon, neh? He must wait for the proper time, as the bosatsu said. And someone must protect you from Old Blowhard—that ghost won't be appeased so easily, I am sure of that. I don't think old Dentō knows enough to keep you entirely from harm. I suppose I had better stay nearby. For a while. Just in case."

Between my sobs, I managed to say, "Thank you." I glanced at him with tear-filled eyes, but I could hardly bear the tenderness of his gaze, and I had to look elsewhere.

Twice, he started to say something and then stopped. I felt his hand gently touch my sleeve. And then he jumped into the air and flew away.

> The Buddha tells us
> we cannot help but suffer
> if we have desires.
>
> But why must it be so?

Rebirth

Does the new moth ask,
drying its wings in the sun,
"So, what am I now?"

$\mathcal{A}$T DAWN, I sat on the veranda facing east. Around me, Dentō had drawn a circular mandala with ashes and other powders. This was not an ordinary ceremony for the initiation of an ubasoku acolyte, I was told, because of the extraordinary circumstances surrounding my decision. Even so, it is not permitted that I describe all that Dentō did.

I will say only that, among other things, he chanted several sutras and performed incantations with incense and sakaki branches, and then he cut my hair. Not all of it, for I was still only an acolyte, but so that it came just below my shoulders. As he cut the strands, he said, "You should give thought to what your new name will be. You need not choose it right away. Often one chooses a thing or quality that one would wish to learn or emulate. Such as my name, Dentō, "tradition," which

I chose because I wish to continue the traditions of my ubasoku ancestors."

My head felt strangely light after the hair was cut. Dentō gathered the cut strands and wrapped them in some cloth. Then I bathed myself and dressed in plain kimonos such as servants wore. When I rejoined Dentō, he handed me a plain walking staff and said, "From now on, you will own nothing but this and whatever you can carry on your back."

For a moment I was reminded of the old woman at the river, demanding my clothes. As a beginning ubasoku, I was allowed more than the truly dead, at least.

I had not yet seen Sōtōko that morning, and I wondered if I would. I had told Sōtōko, during the night, what I was doing and why. She became very upset, railing at me about how I was deserting the family and my duty to have children, and many other hateful things that I shall not repeat. I do not think she believed my explanation about Lord Chomigoto and Emma-O. She accused me of having been perverted by the tengu. I told her that tengu care nothing for monks, but she did not listen. At last I saw that it was no good trying to explain, so I left her chambers and heard her weeping softly behind me.

As Dentō and I were preparing to leave for Heian Kyō, I delayed a little while, hoping Sōtōko would at least come out to say good-bye. She did not. But one of her servants met us at the gate, bringing a small bag that contained some rice cakes, a few coals, and a little brazier.

I tied the bag across my back and said to Dentō, "It would seem my sister does not hate me after all. But I wish she had come out herself to say good-bye."

"Let her grieve your passing in her own way. Families often react so when a beloved member joins an order, and it is right they do so, for that relative can never be the same to them again."

We walked down the Western Road, my feet scuffing in the dust. My legs were still sore from my running the day before, and I could not possibly see how I would manage to trudge the many miles back to the Capital. Yet, without my long hair and with the lighter, simpler clothes, I felt so...unencumbered. Free. The very act of walking was so much easier. I began to understand why Suzume decided not to go to Court.

"Hey ho!" My thoughts were distracted as a big black tengu alighted in the road in front of us. At first I hoped—but, no, it was Kuroihane, not Goranu. "Walking back to the city, old man?" he said to Dentō. "I don't think you can make it at your age."

"Good morning, Kuroihane," said Dentō, bowing. "It has been many years, hasn't it?"

"It has, old man, yet you disappoint me. I see you have remained a monk."

"You do not disappoint me, Kuroihane, for I see you are the rascal you always were."

"So glad to meet your expectations. And who is this woebegone creature with you? Surely this cannot be the Great Lady Mitsuko?"

"Fujiwara no Mitsuko is no more," I said, bowing to him. "I am now the acolyte of this Esteemed Master."

"Ha hoo! Come down a bit in the world, haven't we?"

"She has not so much come down in it," said Dentō, "but is leaving it for a better one."

"Ha! We'll see how she feels when she gets back to the Land of the Good People."

"Yes, well," said Dentō, "if you will excuse us, old friend, we have a long way to travel and some urgency in our business, so we should be moving on."

"Oh, no, no, not so fast, old man. I can't let you be so foolish as to wear down your legs. I could not bear to think

I had wasted the many hours I spent on teaching you." Kuroihane stuck his beak into the air and made a strange call, "Hei-kakakakak!"

Four other tengu flew down from nearby trees onto the road. They carried between them a net I had seen before.

"What is this?" asked Dentō.

"They are going to fly us to Heian Kyō!" I said, happily.

"Are they now? Well, I don't know," Dentō murmured, his chin in his hand, looking dubiously at the net.

"Your little monkette has it right," said Kuroihane. "Prince Goranu's orders. We won't take no for an answer. Now hop in. Your carriage-of-the-air awaits."

As Dentō and I climbed onto the net, I asked, "If you please, Kuroihane, how is Suzume? Has she gone back to Heian Kyō?"

The other tengu began to snort and snicker, and it seemed, beneath his swarthy skin and dark feathers, Kuroihane was turning red as beets.

"She asked about your girlfriend, Kuroihane!"

"About your little ladylove."

"Aren't you going to tell her?"

"About your little nest in the forest?"

"Shut up!" cried Kuroihane to them. He glared at me and spat out, "Suzume...is...fine!"

To quickly change the subject, I asked, "And how is Goranu, and where is he?"

More titters and snickers arose from the other tengu.

"Oooo, somebody else is in love."

"How she misses her Goranu so."

"She dreams of sleeping on black feathers, too."

"Even though she's going to become a monk."

They seemed to find this the most amusing and were laughing so hard, they dropped the edges of the net and rolled on the ground.

"Stop that!" I said. I felt my face grow hot, and I'm sure I was as red as Kuroihane. Perhaps another reason mortals and tengu do not mix is that we poor mortals would be quite unable to withstand the teasing. Dentō politely pretended not to hear.

But the tengu only laughed more at me. "Oooo, touchy, touchy, touchy!"

Kuroihane frowned at me as if this were all my fault. "If you must know, Goranu is back at the Imperial Court, clearing the way for you, or so he said."

"That is...good," said Dentō. "I hope. We did not ask for his help, but I suppose it will do us no harm."

"I don't know why he bothers, old man," grumbled Kuroihane, picking up one end of the net.

"Yes you do, Kuroihane!"

"Goranu wants to impress her."

"Pebbles and twigs for the nest, you know."

"Enough!" roared Kuroihane. "Let's go."

Still chuckling and clattering, the other tengu picked up their edges of the net and jumped into the air. The net jerked up with them, such that Dentō and I bumped into one another.

"Please excuse me," I said.

But the old monk hardly noticed. He was staring out over the trees, saying, "Oh my. Oh my. Oh my!"

"Is this the first time you have traveled this way, Dentō-san?"

"What? Yes. Oh my!"

I almost laughed at his whoops and exclamations, but I did not wish to be disrespectful to the one responsible for my new life. I said nothing further but enjoyed the sight of the hilltops and rivers shining in the morning sun.

The tengu set us down a mile or so outside Heian Kyō, so that our arrival would be seen by few people. The one or two rice farmers who noticed our landing would have unbelievable stories to tell their families. We waved good-bye to the tengu, and Dentō and I set out on our own.

We had to hike some ways down a rough rural path until

we reached the Great Road, the Tōkaido, where we joined the already busy traffic of merchants and peasants heading into Heian Kyō.

It was very strange, entering the city on foot with no carriage around me. I felt quite naked. It was difficult to accept the fact that some men stared at me. Stranger still was that many people did not notice me at all. I was jostled and ignored as if I were no better than Suzume. I wanted to berate those who elbowed me, but I held my tongue. I could no longer be the imperious Mitsuko. I noticed that Dentō accepted the pushing and shoving with humble dignity, and I tried to do the same.

We entered by the eastern gate, which brought us into the city quite close to the Imperial Palace. We went by side streets, and suddenly I stopped, my gaze caught by a familiar white stone wall with a fine, high gate.

"What is it?" asked Dentō.

"My father's house," I said, softly.

"No, you are mistaken. That is Lord Fujiwara's house. He once had a daughter named Mitsuko, but she has disappeared. We have nothing to do with this place."

"But, couldn't we . . ."

"Couldn't we what?"

"Just . . . talk to him?"

"And tell him what?"

"I do not know. Perhaps we could make up something . . . tell him I was killed by wild animals or taken to heaven by a bosatsu."

"You would lie to the Great Lord Fujiwara? The pain such lies would cause you both would be tremendous and unnecessary. Remember, he is still a powerful man. If we pretend to have news of his missing daughter, there would be questions, inquiries, suspicions, perhaps imprisonment. No, no, leave him to his innocent grief. It is better for all concerned."

I scuffed my feet in the dirt. "Sōtōko might tell him in a letter, anyway."

"She may. But our business here will be done, and we will be long gone by the time such a letter arrives, so that will be no danger to your new life."

The gate opened, and one of the guards glared out at us. "You there! What are you loitering around here for?"

"Forgive us," said Dentō, bowing, "but my, um, niece was just admiring the pretty house."

"This neighborhood is not for the likes of you. If you do not have business here, move along!"

"Yes, sir. Come along, niece." Dentō tugged at my sleeve, and I followed him, sadly, down the street.

"How could that guard be so rude to you, a holy man?" I asked, at last.

"He was doing his job. I might have been a thief or some other rogue dressed as a holy man. I do not blame him."

"What a suspicious way to view the world."

"Ah, my dear, you have much to learn." Dentō said nothing more until we reached the smooth, high wall of dark wood and gray stone that marked the boundary of the Palace grounds. Dentō stopped by a small gate set into the wall.

"This is not the proper entrance," I said.

"Not for Those Who Live Above the Clouds," said Dentō. "It is an entrance for servants, soldiers, and lowly folk like us."

I was about to complain about being called lowly folk when the little gate opened. Goranu in his Imperial Courtier-form, except that his robes this time were green, stepped out.

"Ah, there you two are," he said, in a slightly sneering tone. "I am glad you did not keep me waiting long."

Despite his attempt to act aloof, my heart fluttered joyfully to see him. "Why are you dressed as a Third Rank noble?" I blurted out. "You were First Rank before."

"Good morning to you, too," said Goranu. "I see some things about you haven't changed. Yet. I believe your former sister Great Lady Fujiwara no Amaiko knows just about all the First Rank nobility at the palace, so I doubt I could fool her. However, a lowly third ranker might have escaped her notice, neh?"

"Oh. I see. Yes, that was clever of you."

"Would you expect less of me? So. Come in, come in. Mustn't keep the Good People waiting."

We entered. It was all I could do to keep walking and not stare at the beauty around me. The Imperial Palace, truly, is another world. The gardens were beautifully kept, with little streams flowing beneath tiny bridges, past chrysanthemum beds and carefully trimmed pine and cherry trees, disappearing and reappearing amid the buildings. White sand was strewn and raked to resemble coastlines, with the rocks known as mooring stones placed on the sand to resemble mountains or sailing boats. The eye was delighted no matter where one looked. The simple but beautiful wood corridors and bridges were spotlessly polished. People walked quietly, dignified, and now and then we would pass a bamboo blind where just the edges of some Lady's elegant sleeves would be showing, and just a hint of her perfume would waft out to us. *That could have been me*, I thought, *had I chosen this life*.

As I paused to gaze upon a particularly lovely garden of chrysanthemums, Goranu whispered to me, "Remember, all this will pass. It is only a dream. Sooner than you know, all this will fall to ruin and nothing will remain."

Truly, the tengu do not appreciate beauty. "And no tengu will mourn its passing," I said.

"Of course not. That is why we are superior to mortals. Come along."

We were led to one of the women's wings of the Palace, though not the one used by the current wives and female relatives of the Emperor. I remembered having been there once before, long ago. But the Palace is such a maze, I could not have found my own way around.

We were not allowed into the main room itself, but had to wait out on the veranda beside a closed bamboo blind while Goranu went inside. And we waited quite a while. I confess I began to fidget with impatience, while Dentō knelt with eyes closed, perfectly calm and still.

At last we heard someone approach the other side of the bamboo blind. Goranu emerged from somewhere else and came around to join us. "Great Lady Amaiko honors us with her presence," Goranu said.

Dentō bowed low and, reluctantly, so did I. How much I wanted to shake the blinds and say, "Amaiko! It is me! Your little sister!" But I did not.

"We thank the Great Lady," said Dentō, "for agreeing to speak with such lowly personages as we are."

"Good day to you," said Amaiko, her voice as pleasant and cultured as ever. "Lord Atamasaru has made your skills known to me, and I confess I am curious as to why you would be so interested in my family's troubles."

"My Lady may not remember," Dentō said, "that I had occasion to be of help to your family two years ago, in Tamba Province. I have since followed the fortunes of your illustrious family with interest and wish to continue to offer assistance in any way I may."

"Two years ago. Ah. Yes. I prefer not to speak of that time. Or even think of it."

I stared at the blind, shocked. She would forget all that I went through to help her? How could she?

"Then I beg my Lady," Dentō replied, "to forget I have even mentioned it."

"You are forgiven, of course. But Lord Atamasaru has told me of your curious theory that Lady Kiwako is possessed."

"There can be no doubt of it, my Lady. Only a treacherous spirit who has no concern for the body it possesses could engender such foolish behavior on the part of a lady so nobly born. She doubtless knows that she could better her position in life were it not for her... problem. It surely must be that she cannot help herself. Therefore, if we can drive out the cause of this foolishness and enjoin her to protect herself against it ever returning, then surely she can be forgiven and become eligible for the position she so rightly deserves. If I may humbly say so, I am skilled in exorcisms of this nature, and if we can apply this method to your sister, I have no doubts of its success."

"Ah. I see. Yes, that is an interesting theory. It is certainly worth a try. I will speak with Lady Kiwako and see if she is agreeable. Please return tomorrow, and I will tell you if we can put your theory to the test. I will have you lodged nearby so that I may call upon you quickly."

"I thank the Great Lady for the opportunity to again be of assistance."

Suddenly, I became aware that Amaiko was peering out at me through the blinds. "That girl with you. Who is she? Something about her is familiar, though I cannot imagine where I might have seen her."

My hands clutched one another, and I am sure my heart beat so loudly she must have heard it. Yet I said nothing.

"This is my acolyte, who also serves me as a medium, Great Lady."

"Ah. Tell me, girl, have you been to Court before, as a servant, perhaps?"

It took all my will, but I changed my voice to speak like Suzume. "The Great Lady flatters me. No, I haven't served here."

"Ah. I must be in error, then. Good day to you both. Lord Atamasaru, I would speak with you further."

"There is something the Great Lady wishes of me?" Goranu asked, nervously.

"Yes. I am curious as to what sort of business the Office of the Hour of the Monkey conducts."

"Ah! My Lady brings joy to my heart. It is a relief to be acquainted with someone possessed with such intellectual interests as yourself. I rarely get the chance to tell anyone about my work, for no one seems to want to hear about it. I look forward to the many delightful hours it will take to explain all our meticulous record keeping, note taking, and paperwork to my Lady."

"Ah. Well, if it will take some hours, then perhaps we ought to put it off until a later time. I would not think of taking you away from your important business for so long simply for my amusement."

"Oh, it would be no trouble at all, Great Lady! It would be best, however, that you let me know a day or two in advance so that I may gather all the necessary materials to show you. You simply must see examples of the hourly, daily, monthly, and yearly records in order to understand it."

"That is quite all right, Good Sir," Amaiko said. "I could not think of putting you to so much effort for my sake. If you will now excuse me, I have some business of my own to attend to. Good day to you all." With a whisper of fine silk, I heard her leave the blinds and depart.

A deep sadness flowed over me, and I followed Goranu and Dentō out through the hushed, polished corridors without speaking.

"What is the matter?" Goranu asked.

"She didn't recognize me," I whispered.

"Of course not. She wasn't expecting to see her sister dressed as you are in the company of an old provincial monk like Dentō. You mortals rarely see things if they are out of place. Besides, the Good People don't really know each other very well. They do all they can not to. Intimacy is beneath them."

"That is cruel," I muttered.

"Truth often is," he replied.

Goranu led us across a Palace courtyard to some simple buildings that adjoined the outer wall. "You will be lodged here," he said, curtly, "to await the Great Lady's summons." With brief glances at me and Dentō, Goranu spun on his heel and walked away.

I watched him go, wishing I could have asked him when I would see him again. I felt Dentō's hand on my shoulder.

"He cannot take too much interest in us," Dentō said softly, "if he is to keep up appearances. Come, let us see our lodgings."

Our room was next to the kitchens and reeked of cooking smoke. As we ate a plain meal of rice and vegetables, servants would come and go around us, paying us little mind. They used coarse language and laughed too loud. One woman staggered through, clearly drunk.

"I have never seen such sordid people," I said to Dentō.

"Do not be quick to judge," said the monk. "You know nothing of their life, and there are many more like these than like Those Who Live Above the Clouds. These sorts will still be numerous and thriving after noble families have fallen."

"But why? Surely such lives cannot be pleasing to the Great Kami or the Amida."

Dentō paused in chewing his rice and said, "Sometimes I think that the Great Kami did not create mortals with thoughts toward perfection. Rather the opposite. They made mortals more and more contradictory and flawed and unpredictable, until we have become an enigma that cannot be solved. This way, the Great Kami have endless entertainment. They can watch us forever and rarely see the same story twice, and never quite know the end. The Amida Buddha, of course, came among us to teach us how to be free from the kami's meddling, so that we can escape behaving foolishly for their benefit."

Dentō's philosophy was truly different from what I had learned at Sukaku Temple. "What a distressing vision of the world," I murmured.

"Then forget I said it. Think of it only if it is useful to you."

"But, then, how will I know when you tell me what is true?"

"Why should you know what is true?"

I found I could not answer him, and I stared numbly at the floor.

An ugly young man sauntered in and noticed me. "Hey! A new girl around here. Where are you from, little cherry blossom?"

I did not wish to encourage him, so I said nothing and did not look at him.

"What? Think you're too good to speak to me, do you? Hey." He leaned close and made a suggestion I shall not repeat.

"You must forgive her, young man," said Dentō. "She is my acolyte, and she seeks to find the path to leave the world, not to become more worldly."

"Wha? Feh, what a waste. You sure you don't want some of this, girl?" He made a rude gesture I shall not describe.

"I would be careful with her, if I were you," said Dentō mildly. "I chose this one because she makes an excellent medium. She is exquisitely sensitive to the presence of spirits or demons. For all I know, she may be possessed at this very moment. Let us find out, eh?" Dentō pulled a sakaki wand from his bag and tapped me on the shoulder with it. "Demon, if you are within, show yourself!"

I took the hint and immediately began making rough noises and rolling on the floor. "Why have you summoned me, old man?" I growled as I had heard the oni do. I frothed at the mouth and tore at my hair.

The young man stepped back, horrified.

"We wanted to see if you are present," Dentō said.

"I do not want to speak with you!" I shouted. "Leave me

alone!" I shook my head wildly and gnashed my teeth and tore at the reed mats with my fingers.

"Very well," said Dentō. "You may subside." He again tapped me on the shoulder with the wand.

Instantly, I sat up once more and became very still, staring at the floor, saying nothing.

"Uhhh, thanks for the warning, old man. You can have her." The coarse young man hastily left the room.

"Well done," said Dentō softly.

"Thank you," I replied. "I suppose it is practice for tomorrow. Besides, Goranu once told me that dignity can be a hindrance sometimes."

"Surprising wisdom, for a tengu."

I did not chastise Dentō, though I wanted to.

It was difficult to sleep that night amid the smells, and the noises the kitchen servants made, and the rough mats we were given to sleep on. From his snores nearby, Dentō seemed to be sleeping quite well. But I could not help dwelling on how Amaiko had not known me, how I had lost respect and dignity, how I had lost my hair. A little voice wailed inside me, "What have I *done?*"

No answers came, and by the time morning arrived, I felt utterly wretched.

A long scarf of exquisite blue silk was delivered to Dentō, along with the note:

> Great Lady Kiwako is willing and we
> are most eager for your help. Come at once.

No garments were brought for me, and I said, "Surely, Sensei, I cannot go to the Great Ladies' ward looking as I do."

"No," he agreed, squinting his eyes. "You should be a bit more disheveled." He pulled some strands of my hair to hang in front of my face. He tugged at my plain inner and outer kimonos until they hung wrong. "There. Now put on a dull stare and stagger as you walk, and you will resemble a proper medium."

My life had already gone beyond all reason, so what could I do but obey him?

Dentō draped the blue silk over his usual gray robes and, with an air of quiet dignity, he headed across the Imperial compound with me in tow.

We were escorted into the main hall of the Orange Blossom wing of the women's quarters. Though both men and women were hidden behind tall blinds or curtains of modesty, I could hear their excited whispers as we entered, as if they were about to see dancers or some other performance. If Goranu was among them, I could not tell. It was quite possible that my father and sister were among the watchers, as well as Prince Komakai. For once I did not want to shout out who I was, as I wanted no one to know how wretched I had become.

Dentō guided me as if I were a child without control of my own movement. He had me kneel down near the center of the large, open pavilion. Directly across from me was a low, square platform, on which stood four curtains of modesty. Through the spaces between the curtain frames, I could see Kiwako. For once, it was I who could hardly recognize her, she had grown so. Her face had become quite pretty, though she had used too much white powder and had painted her eyebrows too high. Her kimonos were beautifully arranged, though the neckline was perhaps a little too open. Her gaze darted from right to left, and she toyed anxiously with the fan in her hands. She stared at me once, briefly, then looked away.

Dentō stood beside me and began, "May the blessings of the Amida be upon this noble house and all who dwell herein Above the Clouds. I come because one among you, I have heard, is troubled by mono no ke, ill-meaning spirits, that cause her to exhibit unseemly behavior. By the rites of exorcism, it is my intent to drive these spirits from the unfortunate victim's body into this girl who is my medium. There the demon will show its nature, and we will then drive the creature away permanently."

Dentō placed candles at the four corners of the platform and lit them. Black, clove-scented smoke rose like thin pillars from each of the candles.

Then Dentō knelt in front of me and handed me a slender, polished sakaki wand. I took it in both hands. Then he shut his eyes tightly and began to chant the Magic Formula of the Thousand Hands.

Kiwako, on the platform, gracefully fell over in a faint, though I do not know if it was real or she was pretending. The smell of the smoke and the drone of Dentō's chanting produced an eerie feeling in me, and I felt my hair begin to stand on end. *What if we somehow summon real spirits?* I wondered fearfully. *Mama-chan once said that one should never mention the mono no ke in jest, for they might show up for real. What if Lord Chomigoto is watching and sees an opportunity?*

Dentō picked up a sakaki branch and tapped me on both shoulders with it. This was my signal, and I had no choice but to pretend I was possessed. I fell over on the floor and growled and snarled and said the most terrible things. I tore at my clothes and pulled at my hair and kicked with my legs.

Dentō chanted more mystic incantations, louder, and I began to scream and moan as if I were in pain. I was so distanced from myself from lack of sleep, that dignity no longer meant anything to me at all. I was able to scream out my sorrow at the loss of my former life and all I had known, and I am sure I was quite convincing as a tormented demon.

After about an hour, Dentō, frowning with concern, ceased his chanting and tapped me once, then twice more with the sakaki wand. "Malevolent spirit, leave this woman and return to the realm of ghosts from which you came!"

I immediately stopped all of my noise and sat up. I gathered my shabby kimonos around me and looked here and there as if I did not know where I was. The nobles around me gasped as Kiwako also sat up, behind her screens. She began to softly chant the Lotus Sutra in so humble and charming a voice that it seemed her nature truly had changed.

A servant came up to us then, bearing sake and offers to stay and have a meal with the Fujiwara.

Dentō declined the invitations. "Forgive us, but given the volatile nature of that spirit, we should leave immediately. My medium is quite sensitive to their presence, and she might be taken advantage of. Better we should depart so that such opportunistic spirits cannot infect anyone else in the Palace."

And so again I put on a dull stare and staggered as we were escorted—by someone who was not Goranu—from the Palace, back to the little servants' door.

As soon as we were outside the Palace wall, I asked Dentō, "Do you think it will work?"

"If the Good People wish to believe it, and have need to believe it, it will be true for them. People will often grasp at whatever reason, however preposterous, if it will permit them to do what is right or necessary, such as forgiveness. Sometimes it takes a bigger excuse to do the right thing than to do a wrong thing."

The gate in the wall behind us opened again, and a servant came out. He handed a bag to Dentō and a note to me. The note was in Kiwako's hand, and read:

> So,
> *the little puddle*
> *has hid under sakaki leaves.*
> *But I know she's there.*
>
> *May good fortune follow you.*

"She knew it was me," I whispered.

Dentō snatched the note out of my hands and tore it up, scattering the pieces to the wind. "No ties to your former life, understand?"

Tears filled my eyes as I watched the pieces float away. "Dentō," I said, "I no longer understand anything, and the world is a complete confusion to me."

"Congratulations," said Dentō, smiling. "You are well on the path to becoming an ubasoku."

The End of Things

Almost home; warm lights
beckon ahead, but still the
road between is dark....

CHERE REMAINS little of my story left to tell before the end. And yet, how can I say it has an end when every end is also a beginning?

The bag Dentō was given as we left the Imperial Palace contained silver. He used a bit of it to buy us a few days' worth of food. The rest he promptly gave to the nearest beggar. When I protested, he explained, "Wealth is a strong and demanding kami, whom I choose not to serve."

We left Heian Kyō that very day, staying in a dilapidated inn just outside of the northern gate of the city. The wind blew in through the torn paper walls, and there was constant noise from the drunken men on the floor below us. As I picked at my rice and vegetables, I said, "Why haven't we seen Goranu? I wonder why he didn't come to talk to us at the Palace gate?"

Dentō gazed at me, and I think there was pity in his eyes. "It is clear that, although you have promise as a pupil, you are still bound by the Chain of Causality."

"What is that?"

"It is the philosophical chain that binds mortal souls to the Wheel of Rebirth. It has twelve links: ignorance, action, new inclinations, awareness, individuality, the five senses, contact, sensation, desire, attachment, rebirth, and death. I expect you can guess which links particularly bind you."

"It is true." I sighed. "And despite how my life has changed, I cannot see how I will ever be free of them."

"I cannot tell you," said Dentō. "You will discover it yourself. Or not. In this creation of a new life for yourself, you will eventually decide what is the best path for you to take. You may discover your mountain of enlightenment lies in a place unvisited before. And, as all explorers know, in uncharted territory it is necessary to cut a new path."

I was not certain that I understood him, for I was very tired, and the day had been exhausting. I confess, despite my lowly surroundings, that night I slept very well.

By foot, Dentō and I traveled back up the Western Road toward Tamba Province. I was somewhat afraid, given the bad fortune that had befallen my family on that road two years before. But no one bothered us. We even encountered a band of warrior monks from Mount Hiei. But they only bowed and passed pleasantries with Dentō and hardly gave me a second glance.

"I feel like a ghost," I told Dentō on the third day of our journey. "As if I have no existence."

"That is because you are used to defining yourself by how others react to you. This is natural in the day-to-day world; how people sort themselves out with one another. But you must concentrate on different things now. Once you no longer care what people think of you, you will learn what freedom is."

I could not possibly imagine not caring what others think, but I did not tell him so. I was just beginning to learn how very much I had yet to learn.

Two days later, we passed by Sōtōko and Riko's house, but did not stop to visit. I did not know if I would be welcome, and Dentō wished to continue my lesson of cutting myself off from family connections.

Instead, we turned off the Western Road and went into the forest, where we at last presented ourselves before the ruins of the shrine of Lord Chomigoto.

"It does not seem much changed since the storm," I said, looking at the fallen walls and broken roof tiles. The tomb entrance on the hillside had been sealed again with a large stone block.

"But something has been happening here," said Dentō, peering around. "Look at this. There are many recent footprints. And someone has left offerings."

I glanced where he pointed and saw, off to the side of the shrine debris, a neat row of wooden bowls. Dentō was raising each bowl to his face, sniffing at it.

"What are they?"

"Very strange offerings indeed. This one is powdered chalk. The pale green powder is wasabi—horseradish. This one contains sand. This one is plain rice. If there is a message to be read in these, I cannot see it."

"Who could have left these offerings? Perhaps there is another living descendant you have not heard of who has come to do worship?"

"Not that I know of. Perhaps your tengu friends left them."

"But tengu never worship anyone!"

"True. Then perhaps Lady Sōtōko or Tsubushima no Riko left them."

"After the fear Riko showed when he learned what this place

was, I do not think he would ever return or let my sis—Lady Sōtōko return here, let alone leave offerings."

"Well, then, it must remain a mystery." Dentō stood and took a small brazier and some incense from his bag. He placed these on the stone foundation that had held the shrine, saying, "You understand, I find this task most disagreeable. From all I had heard at my mother's knee, Lord Chomigoto was not a beneficent fellow. Still, it is clearly my destiny, neh?"

"I am so very sorry that I have brought you to this, Dentō-san."

"Oh, I doubt very much it is your fault. It might well have come to pass in any case. Ah, well, let us begin." Dentō lit a stick of the incense and placed it across the brazier. He knelt and said, "Chomigoto-sama, kami of this shrine, I, who am descended from your kin and your clan, come at last to do homage to you."

My skin began to tingle, and I felt a strong foreboding. A wisp of white issued from around the stone block sealing Chomigoto's tomb. "Dentō?"

The old monk did not hear me, or ignored me. "Accept, O Kami Chomigoto, the gift of my service, thereby releasing my acolyte, who was formerly known as Fujiwara no Mitsuko, from her debt."

"Your service," said the voice of Lord Chomigoto, hissing on the wind, "is accepted!"

Suddenly, a flash of white light enveloped Dentō, and he sat bolt upright. I was nearly knocked off my feet by the power released from the foundation of the shrine.

"Dentō-san!" I shouted. "Are you all right?"

The old monk slowly stood, raising his arms up high. "Ahhhhhhhhhhh!" he cried.

"What is it, Dentō-san?"

"I live!" he shouted, and then turned to face me. His eyes glowed with a green light, and his face was suffused with a pale shimmer. It was no longer Dentō. "I have overcome the old priest's magic, and now his powers shall be mine!"

"No!" I screamed and stumbled back. This was a true possession, not like the one Kiwako pretended at the Palace. I had no idea what to do.

"Now I will topple the Yamato and the Fujiwara! You, daughter of the Nakatomi," he pointed at me, "shall become my bride. Together we will found a new dynasty and become the new Emperor and Empress of this land!"

I was nearly frozen with fear. Nothing Suzume or Goranu or Dentō had taught me had been preparation for this. I plucked a sakaki wand out of Dentō's pack and waved it at him. "Begone!" I shouted. "Leave this man!"

"Ah-ha-ha-ha!" Chomigoto-Dentō laughed. "You have nowhere near the knowledge to resist me. I have been gathering magical skill for centuries. Surrender to me, little Fujiwara, or you will see the chambers of Lord Emma-O within this very hour."

"No," I whimpered, still wildly casting my gaze about for something, anything, that might help. I saw the bowls of offerings down beside my feet. I knew rice was sometimes a hindrance to demonic spirits, so I picked up that bowl and threw the rice onto the ground between me and the possessed Dentō.

"Ha!" Chomigoto-Dentō laughed again. "I am no mere mono no ke to be held at bay with rice. I now live, in a body of great power! There is nothing you can do." He stepped upon the grains of rice, uncaring. Stretching his hand out to me, he said, "Touch me and all your fears will vanish. You will serve me willingly, happily, and I will make you my honored queen, venerated by all those we conquer."

Desperate, I looked over at the bowls again. *You respect rank and power too much*, Goranu had once said. I acted like a wild creature, unthinking. I took up the bowl of sand and threw it in Chomigoto-Dentō's face.

He staggered back a moment. "What! How dare you!"

I picked up the bowl of chalk and threw that, too.

"Stupid creature!" He became enraged and rushed at me.

With nothing left to do, I picked up the bowl of wasabi and, as he was nearly upon me, threw it in his eyes and nose.

"Arrrrrrgggggh!" Chomigoto-Dentō screamed, holding his face. "Ungrateful child!" He roared. "Now feel the power of my cur-cur-cur-ka-CHOO!" A bolt of green lightning escaped from his hand, but because of his sneeze, it missed me.

"Run around him!" Goranu called from the trees above and behind me. "Keep moving!"

My knees were terribly weak from fear, but my heart lifted upon hearing his voice, and I managed to get to my feet. I staggered to one side of the shrine foundation and then the other. Suddenly, there were many of me encircling Chomigoto-Dentō, each of the other images looking as real as I was.

"Hold still!" cried Chomigoto-Dentō. "Which one are you?"

"Here!" yelled one of the other images, waving her hand. "I'm over here, you silly ghost."

Chomigoto-Dentō unleashed another bolt of green lightning from his hand that, of course, did the illusion no harm but split the tree behind it in half. "Ah-ah-ah-ah-CHOOOO!" he sneezed even louder.

"Over here!"

"Over here!"

"No, me! Curse me!"

I continued to run back and forth, paying no attention to how tired my legs were becoming, fighting back my fear. To the tengu, no doubt, this was all very amusing, but I was running for my life.

"Aghhhhhhhhhhh!" In frustration, Chomigoto-Dentō spun around, flinging curse bolts willy-nilly, some striking quite close to me. Then he stopped and tilted his face toward the sky. "No...no...ah-ah-ah-" He pinched his nose shut. But he could not stop gasping and at last, eyes squeezed shut and watering in pain, he let loose with a mighty "AHHHHHHH-CHOOOOOOOOO!"

A spray of white substance came exploding out of Dentō's mouth and nose, coalescing into the ghostly form of Chomigoto floating beside him. Dentō collapsed onto the ground.

A chorus of cheers and whistles and clacking of beaks erupted from the trees around us.

"You worthless tengu!" roared the ghost. "You think I am defeated, but you will see. I have more power than you know!"

The stone to Lord Chomigoto's tomb burst out of its hole, and two horse-headed oni ran out carrying loops of shining rope. They flung these over the ghost, saying, "Chomigoto-san. Lord Emma-O would speak with you. Now." Tightening the nooses around Chomigoto's form, the oni dragged him back into the tomb.

"No!" cried the ghost. "No! He does not understand. This is my vengeance. He promised me vengeance!"

As soon as the oni and the ghost were inside, the sealing stone flew up into the air and planted itself in the entry hole.

Goranu said behind me, "Lord Emma-O is stern, but just."

I turned and smiled at Goranu, then I ran to Dentō, who still lay on the ground. "Dentō-san! Sensei! Are you all right?"

He moaned loudly, still holding his face, but he allowed me to help him up to a seated position. "Did you have to throw the wasabi?" he groaned.

"I am so sorry, Dentō-san. I did not know what to do. So I tried everything."

He nodded and patted my shoulder. "Never mind. You did well. You have the makings of a fine ubasoku."

There was a flapping of great wings, and Kuroihane alighted

before us, holding a wet cloth. "Here, old man. You look even more a wreck than usual. Maybe this will ease your runny old eyes."

I took the cloth from the tengu and gently applied it to Dentō's face.

The ubasoku sighed. "Thank you."

"Hey, hey! Pretty good, Mountain Puddle." Suzume came running up to me smiling.

"Thank you," I said, still too shaken to think clearly. "But you mustn't call me that anymore."

"I know, but we don't have another name for you yet. Hey, did you like the weapons we set out for you? Worked pretty well, didn't they?"

"You left those offerings?"

"Yes! We knew Old Blowhard was up to something. The chalk was left in case he tried to attack invisibly. The sand is from the temple garden in Kyomizudera. The tengu had to send me in to gather it myself, since they couldn't enter the holy grounds. And the wasabi just seemed like a good idea."

"Why did you not just warn us before we got to the shrine?"

"We didn't know what to warn you about. And we didn't want to hang around here and make Old Blowhard suspicious and change his plans. We figured whatever he would do, you two could handle."

"I am honored by your faith in me," I said.

Suzume grinned. "Well, now that you're not going to Court, I'm willing to be your servant again."

"Ubasoku do not have servants."

"But they can have friends, neh? Besides, you're not an ubasoku yet. And you will need someone to gather firewood and water while you are studying. And since you need to be trained by tengu, we'll have them around, too. What could be better?"

I looked uncertainly at Dentō. "Can she travel with us? Is that not too much attachment to my previous life?"

"Considering," said Dentō, still wiping his face, "that I will be in poor condition for a while—ai, I feel like that ghost sapped the marrow from my bones—I think we should accept whatever assistance is offered."

I turned to Goranu. "I am so very glad to see you again."

Goranu scratched the back of his head and looked around at the trees. "Well, I couldn't let Old Blowhard get his way and ruin everything."

"Yes. Well. Dentō says that so long as I have a new life, I may choose the path it takes. And I cannot imagine such a path if you are not there with me. Even if it keeps me bound to the Great Wheel for this turn or the next. The world is not so bad, neh? I have so much more to learn, and I am beginning to look forward to learning it. Will you stay and teach me, and perhaps we can think about...other things?"

The snickering and hooting began again among the surrounding tengu.

"Ooo, they're talking lovey talk!"

"Maybe we'll get to see them bill and coo."

Goranu turned and glared at them. "In order to get away from these clattering idiots..." He turned again and gazed down at me. "I will follow you anywhere you ask."

And so, that afternoon, we set off: Dentō, carried in a litter; Goranu; Kuroihane, who thought Dentō needed some more lessons; Suzume; and me. We headed for a place in the mountains where we might begin our new lives.

I have set these words down as a way of putting my past behind me, and for Kai-Lung, so that he might know the rest of the story, and for those readers who might find such a tale interesting, though it is hardly a normal sort of monogatari.

As well, Esteemed Reader, I will give you that same gift that I offered to the dragon Kai-Lung. I will let you choose the ending of this story. Perhaps Goranu and I will find a way to remain together, though it might further increase my turns on the Wheel. Perhaps I will become a learned ubasoku, wandering the mountains with magical powers like the tengu, giving occasional aid to those in need. Perhaps my feet will find the Heavenward Path, and I will join the saintly souls at the River of Death someday. Who can see the future? Choose whichever ending pleases you.

The mountain path forks;
leading high, low, and straight on.
Which way shall I go?

AUTHOR'S NOTE

$\mathcal{E}$ VEN THOUGH *The Heavenward Path* is a fantasy, it is placed within a historical setting. But because Heian Japan is so far away in both time and location, it may be difficult for the reader to know just which parts are historical, which parts are from Japanese mythology of the period, and which parts I made up for the sake of the story.

The Heavenward Path is set in approximately A.D. 1100, a time when the great cultural flowering of Heian Japan was beginning to decline. The Imperial Court had become rigid in its customs, and the nobility, the "Good People," as they called themselves, or the "People Who Dwell Above the Clouds," clung desperately to their status and looked down upon anyone who was of lesser birth.

Mitsuko and her family are all fictional characters, but the Fujiwara clan did exist and held great social and political power. For a time, the Fujiwara clan was second only to the Imperial clan itself, the Yamato, and the Fujiwara held on to this status by often marrying their daughters into the imperial line. However, toward the end of the Heian period, other clans were beginning to assert themselves and gain more political clout at Court, threatening the Fujiwara supremacy. This is why Mitsuko faces the dilemma she does at the beginning of the book.

Noblewomen of Heian Japan could wield some political power, either through marriage or by plotting behind the scenes. But at the same time, they lived closeted lives behind screens or curtains of modesty, dressing in many layers of voluminous kimonos to hide their shapes, and hiding their faces behind their sleeves in public.

The noblewomen's greatest contribution to Japanese culture is their literature, their monogatari. Unlike noblemen, who wrote in the stilted Chinese language of scholars, the women were free to write whatever they pleased in their native language. Much of these writings have survived to this day. Some of them are diaries and accounts of likes and dislikes, such as *The Pillow Book of Sei Shonagon*. Some are stories, such as the great novel *The Tale of Genji*, now regarded as a masterpiece of ancient literature. Some are collections of poems and reminiscences, such as *The Sarashina Diary*. The noblewomen would write monogatari for each other and trade them back and forth, expecting that they would only be read by others like themselves. The closest modern equivalent are what are called "zines"—works written informally for a small audience of readers. But the Heian monogatari give such wonderful insight into the lives of the Japanese noblewomen that I drew upon them heavily as background for *The Heavenward Path*.

There were two religions in Heian Japan: Shinto and Buddhism. Shinto is an animist faith based on reverence of kami, gods or spirits that inhabit awe-inspiring places or persons. Shinto is the oldest religion in Japan and forms the foundation of much of its culture. Buddhism originated in India and was introduced in Japan through China in the middle of the sixth century; it became popular among the Japanese nobility and scholars of the period. Buddhism emphasizes transcendence and turning away from the material world through meditation and the study of sutras, long religious poems. Although these two faiths are very different in beliefs, they coexisted and even blended in Heian culture. Thus those of a Buddhist sect, such as the character Dentō, might still perform Shinto rites. It was not unknown for Buddhists to bless and leave offerings at Shinto shrines with the hope of converting the kami that dwelled there, and Shinto demons often were depicted as guardians for Buddhist temples.

Tengu, the mischievous shape-shifters of mountains and forests, are from Shinto folktales. As with any myth, I had to reconcile many conflicting stories as to the nature of the tengu and select the most consistent. There is no Tengu-Do in the stories; however, it is said that tengu were teachers of master swordsmen and shared their magical knowledge with the ubasoku.

The Kofun culture, known by the enormous grand tombs their nobility left behind, flourished several centuries before the Heian period. Some of these tombs are believed to contain ancestors of the Japanese imperial line, and they remain protected and unexcavated to this day. But those that have been opened are much as I have described Lord Chomigoto's tomb, and some are regarded with such reverence that locals believe kami live within them. It is true that the Fujiwara were once called Nakatomi and that their women were said to have been great healers and sorceresses, a legend that fit perfectly into the story I was telling in *The Heavenward Path*.

For those interested in reading more about the Heian Japanese, I recommend (in addition to the monogatari mentioned above) *The World of the Shining Prince: Court Life in Ancient Japan* by Ivan I. Morris.

Amaterasu: Shinto goddess of the sun.

Amida: One of the names for the Buddha, the Japanese version of Amitabha (which means "Boundless Light").

bosatsu: In Buddhism, a spiritual being who, out of compassion, delays entering nirvana in order to give spiritual assistance to mortals. In some regions, they are worshipped as saints or minor deities.

-chan: A diminutive suffix used between members of a family or loved ones, indicating affection.

daikon: A large white radish usually harvested in winter.

Enoshima (Eno): Formerly an island, now a peninsula on the north coast of Sagami Bay, southwest of Tokyo. In folklore, it was believed there was a cave on this island that led all the way to the heart of Mount Fuji.

Enryakuji: The temple complex at the top of Mount Hiei, founded by the monk Saicho early in the Heian period. Over time, the complex grew to nearly thirty buildings.

Fujiwara: The most powerful and influential clan (other than that of the Emperor) throughout the Heian period. The name means "wisteria."

gimmu: Duty or obligation. Sometimes confused with karma, gimmu also refers specifically to those actions that cause one to earn a better or worse fate in the next life.

go: A game of skill played with black and white stones, similar to the modern game Othello.

haniwa: Red-painted clay figures of men, women, houses, and animals, found in Japanese tombs of the Yayoi period (A.D. 300–600).

hapi: A short upper garment with short, wide sleeves.

Heian Kyō: Modern-day Kyoto, this city was the capital of Imperial Japan from A.D. 798 to 1867, although the actual center of political power shifted from Heian Kyō to Kamakura in 1199.

Jizo: A Buddhist saint or bosatsu thought to intercede for troubled souls before the Judge of the Dead, especially on behalf of children.

kami: Usually defined as god or spirit, kami is that force that produces awe. Often associated with natural features such as mountains or rivers, it also can be associated with persons, weather, buildings, etc.

kappa: A mythological creature with the shell of a turtle, the head of a monkey, and the arms and legs of a frog. They are said to live near rivers and ponds and pull children in to drown them. On the top of a kappa's head there is a hollow filled with water—if the water is spilled, they lose their strength.

karma: An individual's fate, determined by the moral quality of that individual's actions earlier in life or in a previous reincarnation.

kichō: Sometimes translated as "curtain of modesty," this furnishing consists of a cloth hung on a low frame, behind which ladies of the Heian court would sit when in the company of men to whom they were not related or married.

kirin: A creature of Chinese mythology, sometimes described as having a deer's body and a dog's or lion's head, and flames on its shoulders. It is regarded as a divine messenger.

koto: A stringed instrument, usually described as a zither. It is a box with a curved roof over which thirteen strings are stretched. It is played by plucking the strings, either with fingers or plectrum.

Miroku (The Buddha Who Is Yet to Be): The Buddha who is supposed to arrive on earth 5,670 million years after the present Buddha has entered nirvana.

monogatari: A written narrative, sometimes fictional, sometimes historical, or a diary. A common literary form written primarily by noble women of the Heian period.

mono no ke: Evil spirits that were thought to be the cause of illness, both mental and physical.

Mount Hiei: Mountain to the northeast of Heian Kyō, on which was founded a major Buddhist temple, Enryakuji. As the temple complex grew to cover the whole mountaintop, it became more common to refer to the mountain itself when indicating the temple complex.

neh: An interrogative, such as "isn't it?"

Noh: Japanese drama form arising out of a blend of Buddhism and Japanese harvest-song traditions, consisting of chanted poetry and symbolic dances to tell a story.

oni: A demon, depicted either with an animal head or with three eyes and two horns. They are sometimes guardians for temples or great kami.

sakaki: A tree sacred in Shinto belief. Sakaki are planted within every shrine area and branches of the tree are often used in rituals.

sake: An alcoholic beverage made from rice, usually served warm.

-sama: An honorific suffix used in addressing someone of very high status (i.e., "Lord").

-san: An honorific suffix, sometimes used as "Mister," indicating respect.

sensei: Teacher or master.

Shingon: ("Pure Word") A sect of Buddhism that believed that mystery lies at the heart of the universe. It tended to blend the beliefs of Shinto and Buddhism.

Shinto: The original folk religion of Japan and the basis of much of its culture, Shinto beliefs centered around the worship of kami and ancestors.

shōji: Sliding door, usually made of wood and paper.

Shrine at Ise: A major Shinto religious center.

sutra: A long religious poem recited as a part of Buddhist worship.

Tendai: A sect of Buddhism, named after a mountain in China, followed by the nobility of Heian Japan, in which the Lotus Sutra was the primary sacred text.

tengu: In Japanese folklore, a shape-shifting goblin or demon who lives in the forests and mountains. They are said to take the shape of birds or people with very long noses. They are masters of magic and illusion and love to harass monks.

Tōkaidō: A major road connecting the cities of eastern Japan.

torii: A symbolic gateway consisting of two pillars and one or more crosspieces, indicating entry into a sacred place.

ubasoku: Wandering monks of the mountains and forests. They were often thought to have great magical powers.

wasabi: Horseradish, usually in the form of a fine, green powder.